THE *final* CHASE

Jessica Florence

Trisia !
the Route !

enjoy
Jessica Florence

Jessica Florence© **2016**

Editing by Librum Artis Editorial Services

Cover by Sarah Hansen, Okay Creations©

To the Animals who have no voice in this world.

I will be your voice

Chapter One

I don't like dirt, and I don't really have a fondness for animals, either. In my opinion, it was a testimony to my love for my niece, Natalie, that I was sitting at Wild Rescue, surrounded by both. Natalie, who was turning seven, loved animals, and wanted to have a cool birthday party with her friends.

In her eyes, the exotic animal rescue center was the best thing ever. I was just waiting for an animal to escape and eat me. I had bad luck like that sometimes.

Just a few days ago, I was standing outside my salon when a dog peed on my stilettos. I kid you not. The little thing lifted its little leg and leaked on me, then sashayed off with its bedazzled collar winking in the sun. It was traumatizing, to say the least.

"Auntie Cammy! You have to come see this wallaby. You can feed it, too! Come on!" Little Natalie grabbed my hand and pulled me toward the small fuzzy creature. Although, what really caught my eye was the man squatting down next to the fuzz ball. Big, blond, and filled out his jeans and flannel pretty well. My little B-cup boobies perked right up. I could stand to pet *him* a little.

He gave Natalie a handful of some sort of feed and held her hands out to the creature. It didn't look too bad. Maybe I could give this a shot for her.

"Here you go, Mrs....?" The man trailed off, as if asking a question. My, my, he was quite flirty already.

"No Mrs. here. The name is Cammy." I squatted down as best as I could in my tea length dress. It was a birthday party, after all; who didn't want to wear a pretty dress to a birthday party?

"Just hold out your hand," he said, with a hint of a country accent. Ooh, I liked that. My blue eyes connected with his brown. Yeah, I could totally tap that if I wanted to. I held out my hand and he placed some little pellets in my palm. Big hands. I wondered if he was big everywhere.

My gaze drifted down to the little kangaroo-looking thing. I was getting a little nervous. It hopped from Natalie's hand over to mine and sniffed it. I bit my lip, waiting to see if it would be a nice little creature and eat the food then move on, or if it would do something horrible. I felt its little muzzle touch my hand, making me audibly sigh my relief.

"Wallabies are sweet creatures; this one here is named Dundee." The man looked at me, then down at Dundee. Dundee probably wouldn't be slaying any crocodiles soon, but he wasn't so bad.

Then the pain hit.

"HOLY HELL! OW! OH MY GOD, THAT HURTS!" That fucker bit me. Bit me hard. I fell back on my ass, bright pink panties on display for all the little kiddies to see. I didn't care. I might not have a finger on my left hand anymore! I panicked. Somehow, while holding my left hand with my right, I managed to get to my feet.

"I need a doctor! Call the paramedics!" I screeched at the flannel man while he looked at me like I was crazy.

"Let me see your hand please, ma'am." He held out his to me. I looked at him in disgust. He told me that thing was sweet. Obviously not!

"No, thank you. Just point me to where I can find a first aid kit, please." I calmed my tone. I subtly felt that all my fingers were still attached, but I bet that bite broke some skin. I would fix myself up. I didn't need some man in flannel who had dirt covering his shoes tending to my wounds. Yeah, I was not in a nice mood right now. Being bit to hell would turn anyone.

"Just follow that trail to the lodge. Ask for Jake." He threw his hands up in surrender and then turned his attention back to the vicious beast. When I turned to follow said trail, I noticed everyone at the party was looking at me. *Shit.*

"I'm good, just going to the lodge. I have to wash my hands and pee." I avoided the *what the hell* look coming from my older sister and fled towards the lodge in search of a man named Jake.

I passed a tall fence that looked like it went on for a good acre or so. I wondered what lived in there. I got my answer when a pack of wolves ran by. I swear one looked at me like I was a juicy steak, but it could have just been me. I saw a house up ahead with a little sign that said *The Lodge*. It was a two-story ranch-style home. Not really a lodge, but whatever. It supposedly held my salvation.

I stepped up the wooden stairs, my heels clicking as I made my way to the bright red door. I knocked, no reply. I knocked again and called out a greeting. Nothing. Peeking in the window next to the door, I saw a table covered with papers but no one in sight.

Voices hit my delicate ears, and it sounded like they were coming from around the house. I walked along the wrap-around porch and saw a barn. Those voices started up again, so I stepped down the stairs and walked the ten yards over to the red barn. It was cute. I really needed to get that first aid kit.

"All right, let's see if Ole Gemma here is having a foal. Jake, you can handle the exam. I've taught you and this will be good for the future if she is." An older male voice told Jake. *JAKE!* I quickened my pace towards the voice, looking over the wooden fence at the men.

"OH, HELL NO!" I couldn't believe what my eyes were seeing.

In the first second, time seemed to slow. I saw sexy brown hair, a trimmed beard running along a chiseled jaw, and perfect lips. Oh, and one of the hottest bods I had ever laid eyes on. He was lean, but had big muscles bulging from his arms. ;ll

In the next second, that is where everything went wrong. Those bulging muscles in his arms? Well one of those arms was elbow-deep in a horse's ass.

Ass.

Yep, a horse's ass.

Eyes of both gentlemen turned towards me.

"Why do you have your whole arm up a horse's ass?" My injury was forgotten. I couldn't understand what I was seeing.

"We are doing a rectal exam to see if the lady is in the family way," said the older man, who was *not* fisting a horse. I didn't speak. I was still in *what the hell* mode.

"We can feel the uterus this way and determine size and hardness to see if she is indeed pregnant." He tried again. I understood him this time, but still wanted to take a Lysol dip after seeing that. Tearing my eyes away from the horse's backside, I looked at the men.

"I'm looking for Jake. The wallaby bit me and I need a first aid kit." They stared at me.

"Please," I added for sincerity. The one man pulled his arm out of the horse. Thank God he was wearing a very long glove. But still. Ewe.

"I'm Jake. Head into the lodge and I'll be there in a minute. The back door is open."
Back door jokes flooded my brain after what I had just seen, but I held them back. Didn't need to make this moment any more awkward than it already was.

"Uh, good luck with that." I nodded and turned to go back to the lodge. This is what happened when a girl like me went out into the woods.

I walked up the stairs and opened the back door. My mind was still reeling from that experience. The inside of the lodge was cozy, but seriously lacked organization. It looked like someone's home. It was a fairly open floor plan. The dining table, like I had seen earlier, had papers scattered about. The living room had a couple of dog beds on the floor and one sofa. The kitchen was pretty nice, though, with commercial appliances. Someone must spend a ton of time cooking. I was looking around when the back door opened. I turned to see Jake, who had melt-your-panties blue eyes that were looking straight at me.

"I didn't catch your name, Miss?" Oh God, his voice. His voice sounded like rain during a summer storm. Soothing, but powerful. That power ran through my veins, making me shiver. Cue wet panties. I shook my head.

"Cammy. Just Cammy. I need a first aid kit." He took a couple steps toward me. Hello, gorgeous.

"Because the wallaby bit you," he stated. His eyes scanned over me, watching me. It was a little unnerving and arousing. Lord, I needed to get laid.

"Yes." I felt like we were in one of those scenes in a book where the heroine takes steps back while defying the hero, as he stalks towards her, pinning her against the wall. Why? It just seemed intense for such little words.

"May I see your hand please, Cammy?" I won't even dignify the feelings I got from hearing him say my name. I held my hands out to him and slowly unwrapped my right from my left. His larger, tan hands took hold of mine. Tingles shot up my arm and down the rest of me. *Oh my!* Then a tinge of pain entered the picture. My middle finger had a bite mark around it. Nothing serious, but it should be cleaned. Maybe I had been a little overdramatic.

"Looks okay. I'll go get you some hand wipes." He let go of my hand and headed into the kitchen. I took a moment to appreciate the fine specimen of manliness as he walked away. He had a nice ass. His jeans and Henley shirt did not hide what was underneath at all. When he came back, I continued my appraisal. He had nice hair, short and chestnut brown. Not styled. His skin looked pretty good, too. Tan. No freckles. Those eyelashes. Man, I had women in my salon spending tons of money to have eyelashes like that.

"Here. I think you're gonna live," he teased. Normally I would have found that jab funny, but I was still traumatized from everything that had occurred in the past hour. My natural-born defiance reared its cute red head.

"Yeah, well, you should teach your animals not to bite." *There.*

"They're wild animals. Animals can bite. Maybe you shouldn't wear such delicious-smelling hand lotion," he commented back. His eyebrows rose and his lips grew into a smirk. I scoffed. My pomegranate and vanilla hand lotion was a staple in my life. Wait a second...

"Why are you smelling my hands? Are you going to bite them too?" Why I said that was beyond me. Sometimes things just leap out of my mouth and I have no control over it.

"I can; I am an animal, you know." That was kind of hot. I bet this Jake would be an animal in the sack. Wild and carnal. With that thought, I decided he and I were too different. I was sundresses, high heels, and make-up. I didn't like to get dirty. Jake was clearly about the animals, since he worked here. Probably was covered in dirt all day and wouldn't know the first thing about a girl like me.

"I can see that. Quite the little kitten, aren't we? Well, I need to get back to the party. Thanks for the wipes, Jake." I blew him a kiss in true Cammy fashion and strutted out the back door. Back doors were getting quite a lot of action around here, I giggled to myself.

Chapter Two

I woke to the sound of an annoying alarm clock. I was too tired for that shit.

"Turn it off, for crying out loud. You don't even need to wake up this early anymore," I grumbled, rolling back over.

"I'm still trying to figure out why you're in my bed this morning." Rayne, my best friend for life, yawned. I rolled back towards her and opened one eye.

"Cammy Jr. needed me." I closed my eye, attempting to go to sleep even though I knew it wouldn't happen. I heard Rayne chuckle. I like hearing her laugh. Rayne and I had been best friends since our freshman year of high school. Up until six months ago, Rayne was the top female MMA fighter in the world. Now she was pregnant and happily married to her hot stud, Arson, who was a retired fighter as well. He was gone this weekend and I was sort of missing Rayne and our alone time. While I loved Arson, and he was the sweetest, most amazing man I had ever met, he hogged her sometimes. Not that she was complaining, but I definitely was! I needed my bestie time.

"Baby needs breakfast. Want to go get waffles with me, since you're here?" My head perked up. I did love food, and I was so excited now that Rayne wasn't on her training diet for fighting. We could totally be fat together.

"I think I can fit it into my schedule." I slowly sat up, wishing I had some coffee right now. Rayne looked cute in her shorts and tank top. She had me cut her black hair short for the summer. It was a little above her shoulders and she rocked it. Combine that with her little baby bump, and she was adorable. She rolled out of bed and went to the bathroom. Slowly I got up and changed into a cute blue sundress and one-inch sandals. Rayne and I traded places in the bathroom and I twisted my long red hair into a stylish messy bun. Next I grabbed the pink eye shadow to make my blue eyes pop, and finished it off with some black mascara. I hardly ever went out in public without make up. It was just barbaric to even think about it.

Together we left her and Arson's apartment to go get some waffles.

"I think once Arson is back from his trip, we are going to start looking at houses," Rayne mumbled while chewing on her large Belgian waffle with strawberries and whipped cream. Cammy Jr. was like me, an eater.

"Awesome, you guys staying close to the bay or wanting to find some more privacy?" I could see them living in a house on the water, where they could buy a boat and do happy family things together. She finished her bite this time before speaking.

"Not sure yet. I like living by the water. It would be a nice jog with the stroller once the baby arrives."

"Cammy Jr.," I corrected her. It was more of a tease than anything. I remember back when we first talked about her needing to have little babies with Arson, she was so flustered. So, to continue to ruffle her feathers, I kept the name. She rolled her eyes.

"How was the party yesterday?" She went back to chewing and speaking. I shook my head. That baby was making her nutty.

"It was like something out of a movie. First there was a hot guy with blond hair. He was all, here baby come feed this wallaby with me. But the damn thing bit me!" I flashed her my bandaged middle finger.

"Then I flashed all the kids my bright pink panties before running into an even hotter guy with his arm up a horse's ass! Then in the lodge, he is all I'll-bite-you-like-an-animal intense. It was crazy, Rayne." I finished telling the events as they happened and took a deep breath. Rayne had stopped eating and was staring at me like I was insane.

"Seriously?" She thought I would make that shit up?

"Yes, seriously!" I exclaimed.

"Why was his arm up a horse's behind?" she asked curiously. Couldn't blame her, it was a shocker in itself. I explained what the old man told me. I wondered briefly if the horse was preggers. Hopefully Jake got his answer before coming to tend to me. That would suck for the horse, if not. Thoughts of Jake's face ran through my mind.

"I know that face, which hot guy are you thinking about?" She was looking at me with sparkles in her eyes. I could never hold back from her.

"Jake, the horse fister." Sadly, calling him that did not diminish how hot he was to me. Nope, not at all. Something was wrong with me.

"Ah, tell me about him. You said he was all I'll-bite-you-like-an-animal. Details, woman! It's my turn to pester you about men." I was about to remind her that she pestered me about a guy I was dating a year ago, but I didn't feel like going down that path. There wasn't really a reason why Daniel and I didn't work. He was perfect in every way I wanted a man to be, but something was missing. I was lost at a loss to what that missing thing was.

"He's tall, brown hair that you could run your fingers through, light stubble, hot build, strong arms, a squeezable butt and a nice smile." Not that I saw a true smile. Just the smirk.

"Oh, he sounds hot." I nodded, he was.

"But I'm not going to give it a second thought. I have no plans of going back there. He is an outdoor man.

He works at the animal rescue. He is probably covered in sweat, dirt, and animal stank all day. I don't even like to walk around barefoot outside. We are complete opposites!" I huffed. She watched me as I officially stated I was not interested in Jake.

"I'm curious to see how this goes." She sat back in her chair and rubbed her baby belly.

"How what goes?" I was confused.

"You and Jake. Something tells me you will be getting Arson'd soon." She smiled smugly. I laughed out loud, probably disturbing the old biddies sitting behind us. I would not be *Arson'd*. When Arson had shown up into Rayne's life, he left no room for arguments. She belonged to him. She fought it for a little while, but he made her fall for him in record time. Yeah, that would so not be happening to me.

"Yeah, I don't think so. I think those hormones are making your brain mush." She just smiled. That smile made me want to stomp my feet in a toddler fit.

"I will not be Arson'd!" I pouted. There would be no earthly reason for my path to cross Jake's ever again. Like I said, we were completely opposite. Rayne raised her hands in submission but I know she didn't actually concede on her statement.

I moved us on to lighter subjects as we finished eating.

"I have to head to the salon. Need me to do anything?" I asked, as she hopped into her little sedan. She shook her head.

"Nope. I think I'm going to swim in the pool a bit, then hang out. Morning sickness has been hitting me a little in the afternoons." All in all, Rayne's pregnancy was going pretty well. They recently had an ultrasound, but didn't want to know the gender of the baby. Crazy, but I was still beyond happy for her.

"Ok. Catch you on the flip side, hooker!" I blew her a kiss and walked over to Bambi, my orange beetle car. I loved Bambi. It didn't take me long to drive over to the salon.

The salon was something I had worked hard for. Lots of hours spent working for an overly-made-up middle-aged woman, gaining as many clients as I could. I worked so hard for so long, and now I owned one of the hottest salons in Sarasota. I had every type of client, from the super-rich to strippers. I loved them all.

Just last year though, I started to take a back seat out on the floor and started managing my business. I had six hair stylists, four nail technicians, two skin care ladies, and three massage therapists. Yeah, my salon was kick-ass. I should have named it that, Kick-Ass Salon, but knew some old ladies would get their panties in a twist over that. So I deemed it Prism Salon. The inside was decorated with many bright colors. Each station was a combination of pastels to bright blues, pinks, corals, greens, and more. You would think it would be a disaster. But it wasn't. I had someone come in and do it. I can proudly say it looks absolutely fabulous!

I pulled into my parking area, which looked pretty full. As soon as I opened the door, I saw everything was in control. Everyone was being tended to, which was magnificent.

"No worries, all. Your fearless leader has arrived!" I alerted them of my entrance. Most of them rolled their eyes. Obviously I was not an intimidating boss.

"Can I get you anything, Ms. Jennings?" My newest receptionist jumped into action.

"Yes. Can you get me a bull whip, a full leather cat suit, and a hockey mask? I obviously need to toughen up my rep so my employees take me seriously," I asked, trying to hold back my laughter when her face paled.

"Uh." I liked making her sweat a little. Hell, I loved to get reactions out of people. It was either a curse or a gift, the great debate of my life.

"I'm just pulling your dick, babe. I'm fine." I air-kissed her cheek and walked back towards my office. I had to look over the new advertising designs. Something was lacking last time, and I couldn't put my finger on it. But this time, I was going to make those designs my bitch.

Chapter Three

An hour later, I had an epiphany. Realizations like this one don't come around too often. It's the type of epiphany that changes your life.

I, Cammy Jennings, wanted a family.

While looking over the files of papers designed to draw women and men to Prism so they could be turned into beautiful butterflies, I decided I wanted to throw those files away and sponsor a little kids'athletic team. It would look so awesome to have a Prism Salon's softball team jersey. Or a basketball team. And I would have to go to games and support the local team that had my name on their backs.

It was then that I realized I wanted that life. I wanted to be the kick-ass soccer mom that was always on point with her hair. I would rock the shit out of bringing juice boxes and snacks after practices. I wanted a husband to pester, who would love me anyway. I was still undecided on a family dog; it was something I would maybe do for the kid but only because I loved him.

I wanted what Arson and Rayne had. The way he stared at her, as if she was the very air he breathed. They were so in love; it was beautiful to be around.

The thoughts that were running through my mind were making me sad. I had no boyfriend. The last one I had, I dumped, because he just didn't light my fire like I wanted. I was thirty, which wasn't old, but it seemed like my crazy clock was ticking, telling me my ovaries were going to shrivel up and turn to dust at any minute.

I needed to get my mind off my lack of future plans, so I left my office and decided to get my hands in the water and do a few walk-in pedicures. I enjoyed every part of it, from scraping the dead skin off the bottom of someone's foot, to chatting them up about whatever, then painting a pretty color on their nails. It kept my mind distracted.

The next time I looked at the clock, it was closing in on six. We were about to clean up and close down for the night. Tomorrow being Sunday, we were closed, so everyone could spend time with their families or just be on their own. The thought made me depressed all over again. I was heading home to nothing but my pretty apartment.

"Hey, Cammy, want to go to Jackie D's tonight? We could get hammered and do some karaoke," asked Mary, one of my hairstylists. My frown turned upside down really quick. That was one way not to be alone tonight! I was so down with that plan.

"Heck, yeah!"

In the salon, I encouraged us to be more like a family. I've found that I keep employees better that way. They knew I still meant business, but I treated them well and they respected that. There were a few of the girls I could call friends. Mary was one of them. She knew how to have a good time.

I closed up the shop about half an hour after everyone left and went home to change. I cleaned up and dressed in black, wide-legged dress pants and a strapless shirt that hugged my waist. I looked in the mirror. Oh yeah, I was looking like my doppelganger, Amy Adams. Petite, red hair, blue eyes, and elfish features staring back at me. I shot a text to Rayne to see if she just wanted to come and hang out, but she said Arson came home early. She would be one busy lady for the next day or so. Lucky bitch.

Time to get out of my lonely apartment.

Jackie D's was a fun bar with lots of drinks flowing, people dancing like no one was watching, and drunkies doing terrible karaoke covers to hit songs. It was fabulous. I loved to let loose. Mary and I threw back a few shots and were getting our freak on out on the dance floor. While twirling with my arms in the air, my eyes caught sight of something familiar. I stopped and looked towards that something, only to feel my nether regions start to tingle. Jake was sitting at a nearby table, nursing a beer with wallaby man. His eyes were on me. Watching me intently. I wish I could say I was plastered, and that was why I decided to walk over to him, but I couldn't. I honestly don't know what drove me over.

"What's up, animal bitches?" I waved. Blond man was grinning and Jake was still looking at me, his expression unreadable.

"Hey, Cammy, how's the finger?" Blondie asked. I looked at him and smiled, while showing him my middle finger. *Just* that finger.

"It's doing okay, thanks for being concerned. Well, have a good night." I was starting to regret my decision to walk over there. I twirled and walked away quite gracefully, but instead of heading back to the dance floor where Mary was getting low with some guy, I beelined for the bathroom. After doing my business successfully, I exited the bathroom and ran into a hard body.

"Ow! What the hell?" I stumbled back, but big arms wrapped around me, steadying me.

"You have a way with words, *Just Cammy*." I looked up and met beautiful blue eyes, which also had a dark blue ring around the outside.

"I have to be good at something," I shrugged, then bit my lip, feeling unsure as to why his arms weren't letting go of me. I was quite stable. Or at least I thought I was.

"I feel like we should explore this," he announced. I stared at him like he sprouted two more heads. Speaking of heads, I was feeling something pressed against my tummy. Something hard and delicious.

"I don't know what you're talking about," I tried, going for plausible denial.

"I'm an animal, remember? I like the chase and I will catch my prey." He walked us back so I was against the wall with his arms caging me in. Why was this so hot? He was a stranger! Well, sort of.

"I'm not prey. And I don't like to be chased," I countered, even though I'm pretty sure it was a lie.

"Of course you do. Ask me how I know." His head leaned in, close enough that I felt his breath caress my lips. Oh Lord.

"Tell me, oh wise one." My voice was breathy and hoarse.

"You're an alpha, a leader. You need a man who will pursue you for your affections, and who will prove he is the better man overall. A man who will take care of your every need. Hard. Slow. Soft. Fast. A man who gives you the world, while giving you stability. You need an equal. An alpha," he purred and I think I just orgasmed. God, now I

29

know what Rayne felt like when Arson was all "I'm your fucks and flowers." I wanted to jump up on this man's cock and go to town.

"That's where you're wrong, kitten. We are completely different. We wouldn't even know what to do with each other, let alone try for stability. It would never work. But lovely words." It was better for me in the long run. He was hot and wild. He was an animal.

"So the chase begins. Remember my words, sweetheart. The longer you run, the sweeter it will be when I catch you. And I will catch you." Orgasm number two? Maybe? For a moment, we just stared at each other. A sort of challenge, if you will. I was determined to fight this. He was determined to chase. This was going to be interesting, one way or the other. Either we would collide and fuck like animals, or it would end in nothing. I was pretty damn strong-willed. He pulled back, releasing me from his arms.

"Enjoy your run, sweetheart," he smirked. I arched a brow and walked back out towards the dance floor. Mary was still dancing with her hunk of burning love. I pondered if I should grab another drink or dance some more when a bolt of genius hit me. I looked at the table where the boys had been, to see Jake was back at the table. Watching me, of course. That smirk still on his face. Oh, buddy, you have no idea what you signed up for. I strutted over to the karaoke area and told the DJ my song selection. The latest performer was almost done belting out her Kesha song, so I was up next. I felt like doing some fist pumps in the air for what was about to happen.

Chapter Four

As soon as she was done, she handed me the microphone and I hopped up on stage.

"Heyyyyyyy! You guys ready to crank the heat up in this joint?" I was a crowd pleaser, what could I say? People cheered and looked towards me. My eyes found Jake's. Oh yeah, bud, it's on.

"This song goes out to my animal man. All you, kitten." I winked at him. Giggling, I turned my back towards the crowd.

Dramatic flair? Check.

When the beat to the song began, my hips started swaying. When it kicked up a little, I turned and started moving around more, getting those pelvic thrusts started. Oh yeah, I was going full throttle. People had stopped dancing to watch me.

Seconds later, I was rapping out the lyrics to *Bad Touch* by Bloodhound Gang. Yeah, I went there. The other blessing was I actually knew the lyrics, so it was effortless for me to dance and sing the song. My hand crept down my stomach and grabbed my invisible nuts at that moment in the song, while I kept my eyes on Jake the whole time. His face was a mixture of amusement and determination.

Soon, I had the crowd singing that they wanted to do it like the animals on the discovery channel.

Pelvic thrust like nobody's business? Check.

Oh yeah, I was on that stage, giving it my best performance. And I will say I was killing it. Towards the end of the song, I started jumping up and down like the rapper I was, with my hand in the air moving to the beat.

As soon as the song ended, I took a bow, blew Jake a kiss, and took my exit. Which I wish was graceful, but my dance act had apparently shaken those shots in my system like a soda can. Yep. I puked, and tripped down the three stairs. I was a violent puker.

I felt hands wrap around me and hoist me up. We moved very quickly to the bathroom. As soon as I saw the toilet I let it all out. I felt my hair being pulled away from my face but I couldn't care. I was dying. My insides were trying to come out of my mouth and nose. Yeah, I was that puker.

"That was a sight I will never forget, sweetheart." Jake's voice was just behind me. I should have cared that Jake was holding my hair, but I couldn't muster the need to care at the moment.

"Holy shit, Cams! Do you need anything?" Mary's voice was next. I groaned my answer before the next round of liquid came out my nose. Gross.

I laid my head on the seat and closed my eyes. I heard Jake and Mary talking, but didn't care to listen. I was concentrating on breathing in and out. My body went limp, and just before I passed out, Jake's voice filled my head.

"I got you, sweetheart. Always." Somehow, I knew he would, which was frightening.

I couldn't feel my legs. Did I break them and lose feeling as I fell down the short set of stairs?

I reluctantly opened my eyes to the early morning sunlight entering the room. Terrible decision. I felt like a vampire seeing the sun. I wanted to hide underneath the covers and nurse this ugly feeling in my body. I wasn't hungover. No, every scrap of alcohol that was in my body had evacuated the premises. But my muscles, and all the joining parts felt like I put myself through the wringer. It was going to be a sweatpants and T-shirt kind of day. Did I have those often? No. Only the day after Thanksgiving with the family, and days like this.

I tried to move my legs again, but still nothing. My eyes started to focus and my brain started to move its gears.

I was not in my bed at my apartment. The ceiling did not have the mosquito net hanging from it like mine did. I looked to both sides and saw I was in a bedroom, one that was really bare. Off-white walls, one dresser, a closet, and a dog bed. Oh, no. Did I go home with someone last night and couldn't remember? I moved my hands to my chest. I sighed in relief. Still wearing my top from last night. I kept going with my clothing assessment. No pants, but my panties were still on. I couldn't have done anything *too* bad.

I once again tried to move my legs and felt something stir around them. My breathing stopped. Something was on my legs. I looked down but couldn't see anything over the gray comforter I was under. Even though I was nervous as hell to see what was on me, I had to know. Very slowly, I used my arms to push myself up.

I screamed.

I screamed like a teenybopper being chased by Freddy Krueger.

There was a cat laying on my legs, but not just any cat. This cat looked like a miniature cheetah! It had to have been at least thirty pounds! I tore my legs out from under it and leapt out of the bed. It did the same, but with more grace. As soon as it landed, it hissed at me, then it raced out of the room like it was never there. I was having a panic attack. I had no clue where I was. Why was I missing my pants? Who did I fool around with? And why was there a giant cat sleeping on my legs?

That's when a shirtless Jake came running into the room. I was stunned calm for a few seconds. I mean, who wouldn't be, when a body like that was staring you in the face? He was all ripped muscles and tan skin. God, every part of his chest was amazing. I mean, he had little dips and bumps in all the right places. Hubba hubba.

"What the hell is your problem, woman?" He was staring at me. Me? What was my problem? Oh hell no, he didn't!

"My problem! I'd like to ask, what the hell is *your* problem? I'm the one that is in *your* house with no pants on, and a freaking jungle cat trying to keep my legs hostage!" I walked right up to him and pointed my red-painted nail at him.

"Explain yourself," I demanded. Yeah, I was a bad ass. I looked at his face. It really was a shame we were on two opposing sides of this game. He was very handsome. Gorgeous, even. His blue eyes were staring at me, watching me. His stupid amazing lips pulled up into an irritating smile.

"OK, I'll enlighten you on the situation. First, the night started off with you wiggling that ass in front of me. I'd call you a cock tease, but you already know that. Then we had a little chat about the game of cat and mouse you want to play. Then you blessed the bar with your performance of *Bad Touch*, pelvic thrusts included. Last but not least, your exit off the stage included puking your guts out while tripping down the stairs."

Oh God... all of that *did* happen. It wasn't just a bad dream.

"Okay, why am I here? Did we...?" I left the last bit off, I couldn't voice it.

"You don't remember? I'm crushed, sweetheart," he teased. Of course we didn't.

"Oh yeah, now I remember, I couldn't feel your teeny tiny weenie. Hence why I forgot. I was reorganizing my closet the whole time. I decided to go with sorting by color, just so you know." Yeah I went there. What?

"Some women find it cute," he commented with sadness. Oh no, did he really have a tiny peen? Poor man, probably got made fun of in the locker room.

"If it makes you feel better, I've been banged so many times my meat curtains flap with the wind." So not true. I cherished my vagina, so that would never happen. But maybe it would make him feel better.

"I'll remember that for the spank bank." He winked. This conversation had taken a weird turn.

"Okay, back to my question, why am I here?" I took a step back to give us some distance and was relieved when he didn't follow me.

"Mary let me have you. She couldn't carry you around, so I asked if I could take you to my place, that we were friends. She fought valiantly, but only for a few seconds. She said you needed a guy like me, but she made sure to follow us here and watch me put you in bed. She was the one that removed your pants. Sexy panties, by the way. I have a thing for lace." His eyes drifted down to said panties. I wanted to cover myself from his perusal but I didn't. I thought I looked good in my purple lace cheekies.

Mary was so fired. Not really, but I would at least give her bathroom cleaning duty or something.

"The jungle cat?" I had to know, did one of his creatures escape?

"Binksie? He's an African Serval. Rescue. A woman thought it would be cool to have him as a pet but didn't want to put in the time. She dumped him off in the middle of nowhere with his leash tied to a tree. I got the call from someone who saw it happen and went to get him. He's fine now, he's kind of adopted me so now he won't leave the house." Huh, that was an interesting story. I digested all of the information he had given me, but there was still one question that was burning in my head.

"Why are you shirtless?"

"Casey spit up on me so I needed to shower and change." Casey?

"You have a baby?" The thought was oddly surprising.

"No, Casey is a baby tiger. She hasn't been feeling too well."

"Oh, poor thing." We stood there with no words being exchanged. Yeah, I needed to go.

"Well, I'm going to get dressed when I find my pants, and

40

get out of here. Good luck with Casey." I turned and looked around for my pants. I heard a growl behind me, a sexy one. So when I spotted those pants, I made a little show of my walk and bending over grabbing them. Shoving my ass out like a stripper. I was a cock tease and I was enjoying this.

Then rough hands gripped my hips and pulled me back against a very hard, not teeny, peen. I felt my sex instantly start to quiver. I lifted my upper half and was flush against his naked torso. Yum.

"Presenting your perfect ass in the air like a cat in heat, that's playing with fire, sweetheart," he growled into my hair. I wanted him to bend me over the dresser and fuck me hard, but that would be it. It would be as simple as sex—hot sex—but just sex. As a couple, we would never work.

"Not doing anything. You're just a horn dog." I untangled myself from him and slipped on my pants. Totally wishing I had sweatpants.

"I made breakfast, come down the stairs when you're ready." He turned and left. My stomach growled.

Food did sound really good. I left the room in search of a bathroom, which I found just across the hall from the room. So far this house was pretty pleasant. Not overly decorated, very simple. I used the facilities and checked out my face.

"Oh frock," I muttered. I had troll doll hair and my makeup was smeared everywhere. I looked like I belonged out in one of the cages in the rescue. Wishing I knew where my clutch was, with my small bottle of makeup remover, I grabbed some tissues and moistened them with water. I did what I could, which was a miracle, in my eyes. I looked pretty good after cleaning up. Rinsing out my mouth to get rid of the bed breath, I felt refreshed. My stomach growled again, warning me I needed to get some grub.

Chapter Five

I walked down the stairs, toward the sounds of plates being shuffled. Jake had donned a shirt and was placing a few plates on the table, which was now paperless.

"My, my, are we showing off for little old me?" I teased. He didn't reply, but went and grabbed two glasses of orange juice.

I walked over to the table and sat my butt down. Man, did he outdo himself! Eggs, bacon, biscuits, and hash browns. Lord almighty, this man was trying to undo me. I was about to ask if he had made coffee when he set down cups for us both with the pot in between. Sugar and cream appeared moments later. Okay, this was something I could get used to.

"So, Jake, tell me about the man behind the animals." I poured some coffee and spooned in three scoops of sugar. I liked my coffee sweet. His large body sat in the chair opposite of me and made himself his own cup. Three scoops of sugar. Interesting.

"I own and run the rescue. Currently sitting on 200 acres. We take care of all sorts of creatures, including tigers, lions, and bears."

"OH MY!" I couldn't help myself. He smiled at me while I covered my plate with food

"I'm thirty-two years young. Virgo, don't care for walks on the beach. I feel manscaping is a must, and I can make you come in two minutes with my tongue."

Maybe stuffing my face while he talked was a poor decision, especially considering his words made me choke. Yep, red face hacking was underway. Holy hell, was this guy for real?

"Okay then." It was the only comment I had.
"So, Cammy, tell me about the woman behind the rapper." He smirked, then took a bite of bacon. Lucky bacon.

"I own and run Prism Salon on St. Armand's Circle. I'm thirty, agree on the beach walking. Not fun at all. And yes, I am one hundred percent pro-manscaping. No skills in the mouth department, I'm actually a poor lay." His eyebrow raised, obviously not believing me. Not sure why I was lying about my sex life so much to him. I couldn't truly lie to save my life, maybe that's why no one took me seriously. I giggle at the thought.

"Yeah, that's a lie. I'm a fucking pro." At least I was being honest. I could suck a dick with the best of them. A chuckle slipped from his perfect lips before he continued eating. We ate in silence after that, which I was absolutely okay with. After we were both stuffed, Jake was the one to break the quiet.

"I want to get to know you more, and I feel the only way to do that is to win a bet." It was my turn to raise the eyebrow at him. What was he talking about?

"I bet I can paint your toes to perfection. If I lose, you don't ever have to see me again." He looked at me with a serious expression. I leaned in closer.

"And if you win?" I was a very curious kitten.

"If I win, you stay here for a week and help out on the rescue." I scoffed.

"Deal. There's no way you can do that good of a job. I'm a hard critic, so I'll call your bluff." Yeah, I was ready for this disaster. The man was practically a bear himself, a handsome bear. But really?

"Let's get this train wreck over with. I need to get home and into some sweatpants." I totally unbuttoned my pants like the lady I was—a bloated one. Jake noticed my movements then stormed up the stairs.

I closed my eyes, and when I opened them, he was back and standing in front of me with a large T-shirt and sweatpants.
"Uh, thanks." I wasn't going to turn them down. I wanted to get out of last night's clothes badly.

"There's a bathroom just down the hall, no need to go upstairs." He pointed just behind the stairs. Cool. I made haste and changed into the large clothing. I had to tie the sweatpants string really tight and the shirt I tucked the front into the pants, but all in all I looked pretty awesome. As always. Before going back out to see Jake, I needed to have a girly moment with his clothing. They smelled of man. Clean and woodsy. Yeah, woodsy. Wearing his clothes felt really intimate, like he was holding me without touching me. I should have just left. Stupid breakfast. I was starting to like him.

Needing to get out of my head, I left the bathroom and found him in the living room. That jungle cat, Binksie, was lounging on one of the dog beds. It was unreal to see a cat like that, just as domesticated as a normal house cat.

"Have a seat." Jake gestured to the couch in front of him. I strutted over and plopped down on the couch. He hadn't moved, so I looked up at his face. His eyes were moving all over my body. I felt a blush fan my cheeks.

"I like you in my clothes," he commented as he went down to his knees in front of me. Oh, the thoughts that ran through my head. He grabbed a small bottle of red fingernail polish, as well as polish remover. Interesting that he had that.

"Leftovers from a girlfriend?" I asked. He smirked.

"Sisters. They visit every once in a while, leave their shit everywhere." He gently lifted my perfectly pedicured

47

foot and started on his bet. I closed my eyes, wanting to see the finished product with a fresh perspective. The longer he worked, the more the anticipation was building inside me. Realistically, I was perfectly able to stay here and help on the rescue if he won. I was unsure about helping with the animals, and this was way different than the busy downtown Sarasota area, but it might be nice. Keeping my panties on would be hard, though. My thoughts then drifted to having a family and being a juice box mom. I really needed to find a husband and get to baby making. Jake popped into my head, but I squashed the thought. Maybe I should just screw him and get it over with.

His life was not the life for me. I wasn't sure why I was wasting my time dallying with this bet.

"All done. Open your eyes, sweetheart." I opened my eyes, and well, I guess I shouldn't have been surprised. If a man was so sure of himself that he was willing to make a bet, it's probably because he knows he can win. My toes looked really good. Was he as good as me? No. But I would have been satisfied. I sighed.

"I have to go home and pack a bag," I told him. I looked at him just as a bright smile grew on his face. I shook my head. This was going to be a long week.

"I'll take you to your car." I nodded in agreement.

"Wait, what about the animals? Can you leave?" I had no clue about anything that went into an exotic animal rescue.

"I'm the boss. I have thirty employees, ten interns, and about ten volunteers. I think I can get away for a bit." He stood and held his hand out for mine.

"I'm Jake Wild, owner of Wild Rescue." I took his hand and he hauled me up. My body collided with his. Yep this was going to be a hard week.

"All right, big boy, get me to my car, and I'll be back later." I needed some space like yesterday. This man was making my insides go haywire. I wanted him, but I didn't. I did, but I didn't. I was getting whiplash over here. I pulled back and waited for him. He nodded his head towards the door.

"Let's go, sweetheart." I followed, and stared at his ass as we walked towards a dark blue truck with the logo for the rescue on it. It had mud around the tires and a dent or two. Looked like it was used as a truck. I see lots of people drive trucks around downtown, but they probably had spider webs in the back from it not being used for its intended purpose. Jake opened the passenger door for me and held out his hand in case I needed help. I climbed up in the beast all on my own. I was independent like that. I liked the gentleman type but I was too impatient for them. I didn't want to wait in the car while they got out and walked around to open it for me, or wait for them to open the door so I could walk through. I had shit to do; ain't nobody got time for that.

The ride was surprisingly quiet. I welcomed it. Maybe Jake caught on that I needed some space. I agreed to stay at his rescue for a week. It was a big move, especially when it was with someone I really didn't know. I just hoped a tiger didn't eat me. When we pulled up to Bambi, Jake stopped the truck.

"I'll see you later, sweetheart. Dinner's at six." He leaned over and kissed my cheek. Sweet points go to Jake on that one. He wasn't being weird or clingy. I got out and once I was finally safe inside Bambi, Jake drove off. Before I started the car, I sent a text to Rayne.

I'm coming over. Tell hubs he doesn't have to get dressed on my account.

I started my girl up and drove over to their apartment. I needed my Rayne.

Chapter Six

I took the elevator to her floor because only weird exercise freaks like her took six flights of stairs. I knocked on the door, and it was opened immediately by Arson. That man was yummylicious. Too bad he was wearing clothes.

"Cammy, my other half's other half." He smirked and held out a cup for me to take. I looked inside it.

"Oh my God, you're a lifesaver!" I grabbed the cup and sucked on the straw like I was sucking cock. He got me a smoothie. I loved smoothie time with them. I walked in to see Rayne sitting on the couch sucking on her own smoothie.

I let out a moan when the taste of strawberry and kiwi hit my tongue.

I looked at Arson, who winked at me. That man knew me. I loved this flavor combination.

"So, what's up?" Rayne took a break from her drink. I plopped down next to her and rubbed her little Buddha belly. I was the only one besides Arson and her mom that was allowed to do that, so I did it whenever I could.

"I'm being Arson'd!" I whined. It was happening.

"I told you it was going to happen. I so called it." She beamed.

"Being Arson'd?" Arson piped up and sat on the chair across from us. His brows arched.

"Yeah, Arson'd. You just came into my life like "You my woman" and didn't let me think otherwise. You Arson'd me." Rayne explained to him. He shook his head and chuckled.
"So what happened?" she asked.

I started to tell them everything. She laughed and swooned at the appropriate parts, except when I told her about me falling and puking. Then she laughed at my pain.

"I can't believe you sang Bad Touch to him. That is classic." She laughed hysterically. It was the highlight of that night.

"I rocked it." I mentally patted myself on the back, trying to forget the unglamorous exit.

"Man, that was quite a story. He totally did Arson you with that whole *you need an alpha* speech. So hot." That. It. Was.

"Now I've got to let the girls know I won't be in this week, because I'll be staying at his house and helping out on the rescue. Whatever that means." I drank the rest of my smoothie.

"It means you're going to be having 'wild' animal sex. Get it? Get it, wild because his last name is Wild." Rayne was mocking me and my corny jokes. I found it funny, but kept my laughter to myself.

"I don't want to have sex with him. He's too different from me," I whined. Was it a lost cause that I was holding off having sex?

"Sounds like a good guy to me," Arson stated. I looked at him like he betrayed me.

"What? He works hard, stated his intentions upfront, and hasn't tried to fuck you yet. He's waiting for you to get accustomed to the idea first." I thought over his words. What he said did make Jake seem like a nice guy. He was forward with what he wanted with me but he wasn't aggressive. Hmm, food for thought.

"I'm pro-Jake in this quest. Sorry, hon, you need a guy. This is your 'I want one' chance." Back when Arson was trying to win her over, I whined how I wanted one. I wanted a guy to look at me how he did her.

"I still think we're too different," I huffed.

"Maybe different is what you need. Guys like you don't seem to be working," Arson commented.

"When did you two turn into Mr. Miyagi?" I looked at them.

"I learned from the almighty Cammy." She hugged me. When did I turn into such a sap? I hugged her and held on. Rayne was such a big part of my life. I loved her so much.

I stayed over for another hour before heading home to put together a bag for my week.

I called Mary to let her know I wouldn't be in this week. She said it was good and to have fun. I wasn't needed anywhere. So after a shower, vegging on the couch, and three suitcases later, I was on my way back to the rescue.

It was right around 5:30, so I would be there for dinner. I wondered what was on the menu.

There were people all over the place, doing their jobs, as I pulled up to the lodge. I parked Bambi next to Jake's truck and hopped out.

No one was paying attention to me as I hauled my suitcases out of Bambi and started lugging them up the wooden porch.

"Hey there, lady. Let me help you with those." The flannel man from the wallaby incident took hold of my luggage and brought them up the rest of the way.

"Thanks." I huffed breathlessly.

"Name's Derek, by the way." He held out his hand which I shook.

"So why the suitcases?" he asked. I wondered if Jake had mentioned to anyone about me being here.

"Well there isn't such a thing as too many sexy toys, am I right?" Out of all the answers that could have come out of my mouth, I'm not really sure why that one was it. His face turned red. Well, at least making him blush was fun. Just as I was about to say I was joking, Jake walked up the stairs.

"I got this. Thanks, Derek." He smacked the man on the back in a bro type of way before grabbing my bags with ease. Derek, still blushing, muttered bye, and walked away.

"What did you say to him?" Jake's tone was inquisitive. I shrugged and blinked innocently.

"He asked why the suitcases, and I asked him if there was such a thing as too many sex toys. Shall we?" I opened the door and walked inside. Leaving Jake on the porch. In shock. Shaking his head, he walked inside and went up the stairs. I followed behind and noticed he didn't put my bags in the spare room. I followed him into a larger room with a big bed with wooden posts, and crisp, dark blue sheets. There was a dresser and what looked like a walk-in closet just before a door I assumed was a bathroom. By one of the two windows there was a sort of cushioned bench and a dog bed on the floor, for Binksie, I was guessing.

"I'm not staying in the other room?" I finally vocalized my confusion. He set the bags down and looked at me.

"Nope, you're staying with me." I gasped.

"No way! Being here with you is crazy enough. I don't really even know you! I'm not sleeping with you. Plus, I snore! And I'm a bed hog. Just ask my best friend, Rayne. I'm the worst. Really, for your safety I should move into the other room." He walked closer and I took a few steps back. Was it just me, or was Jake prowling forward making me turn on the water park in my panties? Dammit! When my back hit the wall, I knew I was screwed.

His body pressed up against mine, and before I could stop it, a little mewling sound escaped my lips. I watched as his blue eyes turned darker. Oh God, was he going to kiss me?

"I'll take my chances. Your perfect ass is cuddling up to me tonight." He leaned in to kiss my nose and walked out of the room. I sagged against the wall. That man. He did something fierce to me, things I didn't want to be feeling. I looked around the room and then to my suitcases. Fine, he wanted me to stay in here with him; I would make myself right at home.

I got to work on unloading my bags and making room in the drawers and closet. I was surprised to see he had cleared some space for me but then I giggled when I saw how little room there was. It was cute, he really must have thought I wouldn't be bringing too much. As if!

I reorganized his drawers, taking over more than half. And I may or may not have fondled his boxers a bit. Thoughts of him walking around half-naked drifted through my head as I got to work on the closet. After the closet was finished, I went into the bathroom and set up all of my beauty supplies. By the time Jake was calling me down for dinner, I looked around the room and felt at home. Which surprised me. I turned and went downstairs to see what he had made.

Chapter Seven

"Thanks for giving me some space for clothes." I beamed mischievously. He looked at my face, trying to read my expression.

"I have a feeling things are going to be quite different up there, aren't they?" He was spot on.

"You can always change your mind." I fluttered my eyelashes.

"No chance in hell, sweetheart." He set the table with everything for dinner. It smelled divine.

I walked over to the table just as he was setting down some drinks. If this man was trying to win me over, he was doing a good job of making my stomach Team Wild. There were alfredo noodles in a big bowl, a yummy looking salad, and garlic bread that was calling my name.

"I didn't know if you were allergic to shrimp, so I put it on the side." He set down a smaller bowl full of steamed shrimp next to the pasta.

My stomach growled in anticipation. I quickly sat down and poured myself some of the water with lemon that was set out.

"You really like to make meals, don't you?" So far he's gone all out for me with food. I looked up at him, teasing.

"Gotta puff out my chest and show I can provide for my woman." I rolled my eyes. Funny guy, that one.

"Looks good," I commented, as he sat down. Together we loaded up our plates, with shrimp included. I moaned when the noodles hit my tongue.

"Okay, you win. I'll marry you. Just cook for me every meal of the day." I stuffed my face like a pot smoker with the munchies. I did not care if I looked like a total cow as I ate the pasta and crunched through the bread. Pure heaven.

"That was easy," he commented and smiled as he took some bites. We ate in silence for the rest of the time.

Both busy eating. I was beginning to like that little routine. Once we were done, I sat back and took a deep breath. I didn't come up for air much during dinner.

"So, what exactly will I be doing this week? Cleaning poop? Petting kitties? Playing house bitch?" I was genuinely curious about what I would be doing. Jake sat back and looked me in the eyes. Yum.

"Just normal stuff. I'll give you a tour in the morning, introduce you to a couple of the people working here. We'll feed some animals, clean cages, have lunch, pretty much take care of whatever we need to." Physical labor. By the end of this week, I was going to be as fit as Rayne. Well, not really, but I was going to have some serious bicep definition going on.

"Alrighty then." I nodded. I was in, no matter what. Cammy Jennings was no quitter. A whiner? Sure. A little dramatic? Yep. But no quitter. I was down one hundred percent.

"So what now?" I looked around, unsure what to do.

"I have to go back out and take care of a few things, so why don't you just relax? Do the peeking around I can tell you want to do." He smirked. Okay, it was weird that he knew so much about me. I was totally dying to look around the house. I was such a creeper. I wanted to search through every nook and cranny of this place. I raised my hands in surrender.

"You got me there. No worries, that clawfoot bathtub of yours is calling my name." I rubbed my hands together like I was hatching an evil plot.

When I entered his bathroom before dinner, I was stunned to see such a pretty clawfoot bathtub and a large glass encased shower next to it. It was quite luxurious for a ranch- style home.

He simply chuckled and grabbed our cleaned plates, then put them in the sink.

"I'll clean up. The least I could do." I stood and started helping put things away. He helped me find the Tupperware and I subtly organized his big fridge. Everything this man had was big. Big ranch home, big shower, big fridge, big...muscles? Yeah, I wanted to say cock. But I was still unsure about that. I thought I felt something when he went all caveman on me at the bar, but I was pretty knackered. As soon as we were done, Jake left to go do whatever Jake does at the rescue, and I made my way upstairs to start winding down for the night.

I turned on the light and stopped. Binksie the giant cat was lying in my open suitcase that I had left on the floor.

"It seems you and I are at an impasse." I stood tall, not letting him see the nervousness in my eyes. He just looked at me, curiously.

"I'm going to be staying here for the week." I walked slowly towards him, trying not to freak him out.

"Now as you can probably tell, I'm not a huge animal person, but I promise I won't bother you, if you won't eat me at any time during my stay." As slowly as my burning quads would let me, I crouched down and held out my hand to the beast. I took a deep breath.

"If you're going to bite me or something, just get it out of the way now so we can move on and be civil." I closed my eyes, waiting for the pain to occur.

Bump.

My eyes opened to see the cat's head butting my hand. Cautiously, I put my hand on its head and moved it around. My heart was thumping a mile a minute. This was freaking scary as hell for me, considering my past with animals.

It wasn't until I heard him start to purr that I felt at ease.

"Huh, maybe you aren't a vicious creature." I petted his head and scratched behind his ear. Maybe I made my first little friend here.

"If you keep this up, I'll have to sneak you some catnip. Then we can really have some fun." I pulled my hand back and decided to let my new friend hang out in my suitcase. It seemed a little small for him, but hey, that was his choice. I made my way into the bathroom and found my lavender bubble bath that I had the foresight to bring. I turned on the water to my desired temp then added in my bubbles. I watched as they grew into little bubble mountains. Oh yeah, I was going to be submerged in bubble heaven.

I cracked the door so if Binksie wanted to come say hello, he could. I stripped down and stepped into the sweet euphoria of the water. I covered myself with bubbles, because that's what you do in a bathtub. You make a bubble bikini, although I probably looked like I was buried under bubbles. I settled in and cleared my mind. A lot was going on this week.

Chapter Eight

I have no clue how long I soaked in the tub. The bubbles still covered me, but there weren't as many. I was in my own Cammy world of juice boxes and soccer games when the door opened and Jake walked in, shirt halfway over his head.

"Uh, still in here!" I shrieked, trying to cover my goodies up with as many bubbles as possible.

"Oh, don't mind me. Just need a shower." I kid you not, the man just stripped right in front of me. Hot muscles, ass, and definitely not a tiny cock were being paraded in front of me like a damn carrot. Oh Lord, did my nipples perk up, begging to be touched; my pussy ached, and I wiggled a little from it being uncomfortable.

Jake Wild was the man that women's porn was made of. He turned on the shower and stepped in. Thank the shower gods for clear glass. Totally without shame, I caressed myself as he ran his hands through his brown hair, down his face, and over his unbelievably tongue-fuckable body. Those abs, those arms, those legs, that ass! I wanted to take a bite out of it, like chocolate. More than that, I wanted to ride his face and cock like a cowgirl.

When he turned to wash his back, his eyes connected with mine. I could see desire forming in his gaze. His eyes dipped down and I followed the line of sight. Oops. One nipple was not being hidden by the bubbles. I looked back at him to see him staring at me like a damn animal about to pounce. God, that was so hot.

Like the squirrel I was, I saw movement below and my attention was directed to his growing cock. Oh dear God. Jumping out of the bathtub like a bat out of hell, I grabbed a towel and ran out of the room. I couldn't do it.

I wanted nothing more than to jump onto his cock and hold on for dear life, but shit! I was going to stay here for a whole week! I couldn't let my pink velvet sausage wallet dictate what was happening. I was a sore sack of poo right now. I was horny as hell, and frustrated. I wanted him, but he couldn't be my end game. This wasn't my future. I dried off and put on some clothes. I was determined to act like nothing happened. Yeah, I was a wuss.

When Jake finally exited the shower, I was down in the living room trying to figure out his TV set. It wasn't anything fancy, but he only had one remote and I didn't know what the settings were.

"How do you work this thing?" I growled as he came down the stairs. I was too ashamed to look him in the face, so I just stared at the remote. His big hands gently took the remote from my hands and I watched as he pressed a button to the side and the TV turned on. Okay, then.

"Sweetheart." His voice was soft, and was beckoning me to look at him. I didn't. I looked at the TV, but then his fingers gently lifted my chin so I had to face him. The whole bathroom scene flooded my mind. His eyes on me. My fingers on my clit. His cock growing at the sight of my nipple.

69

"What's going through that head of yours?" he asked.

Closing my eyes, I leaned in and softly pressed my lips to his. Immediately, I felt something I'd never experienced. My heart raced, tingles raced through my veins, and stars exploded behind my eyes. We hadn't even moved from just our lips meeting, and I wanted to grip him hard, run my hands through his hair, then throw him on the couch and have my naughty way with him. But, I also wanted this moment to last. I knew my head would catch up soon and scream at me to end this.

I pulled back slightly, only to connect us again. This time we moved against each other's mouths. Teasing. His teeth gently nipped at my lower lip. Wanting to explore more, I opened for him and our tongues danced in sync. His hands gently cupped the back of my head, keeping me close. My hands clenched his shirt, wanting the exact thing. To be close, to never let this moment end. But it did.

Binksie chose that moment to rub up against us annoyingly. I pulled back and came to a decision.

"All right, kitten. You win. I'm yours for the week. I'll try not to over think things, although I won't make any promises." I took a step out of his arms and looked him in those pretty blue eyes. I was a nut for making this deal in the first place, so I guess I was going full loon and embracing the dark side.

"One week," he huffed.

"You might want to relax for the rest of the night. Busy day tomorrow." He set the remote down on the couch and walked off into the kitchen. I sagged onto the cushions as Binksie rubbed up against my legs. Little pussy blocker.

He walked back into the room a few minutes later looking cool as a cucumber, unlike me. My head was all over the place.

"Naughty little animal, aren't you?" He was looking at me with an amused face. I looked at him with confusion. You could tell he was holding back his laughter. What the hell? He nodded his head towards the TV. I just realized I hadn't even looked to see what was on. Oh boy.

Monkeys were getting it on. *Animal Mating Rituals* on the animal channel was on full blast. Cue red cheeks.

"Well, if I'm going to be playing with you, kitten, I gotta learn all the animal tricks." Yeah, I was trying to play it off. He laughed and sat on the cushion next to me.

"Not sure I like the nickname you keep playing at." He didn't move to change the channel. Should I? But then I'd have to cross his body to grab the remote. This couch was sort of large. I bet he could sleep on it pretty comfortably, and he was no small man.

"Name stays. Are you going to change this or are we going to continue to watch animals get it on?" I whined. He looked at me and that smirk rose onto his face.

"You want to change it, there's the remote." He pointed to his right, where the remote was nestled in the corner of the couch, against the armrest. It was probably only four feet away. I could easily get up and get it, but call me a pyro, because I was totally in for playing with this fire. I looked at him and rose onto my knees. Like the kitty cat I was trying to be, I crawled across him, ass in the air. I pressed my face into the couch, successfully placing my ass right in his face, and grabbed the remote.

"EEP!" I shrieked. He bit my ass!

"I told you, sweetheart, all animals can bite," he said to my backside. I knocked his face with my bottom and climbed back to my side.

"Savage," I murmured, and changed the channel. But even as I settled back in the couch, I felt my insides stir, and my core heat up. I apparently liked that love bite. We didn't say anything after that, but my mind was rolling. I thought about the type of sex you would have with a man like Jake. Rough, animal sex, I bet. He would pick you up and move you around. Pound into you from behind and bite your neck as he growled in release. Oh yeah, I bet Jake was a growler.

Chapter Nine

The thought of us, with all my claws and his teeth, had me crawling on his lap and fusing my lips to his. I was burning hot as hell for this man by just the thought of what he could do. I wanted that, right now. His hands gripped my hips, bringing me down onto his growing erection. A growl came up his throat at the contact.

That growl. Oh, I knew it. I ground against him, trying to relieve the ache my thoughts of him had created. My tongue plundered his mouth, feeling and touching every part of him. This kiss was nothing like the sweet "make love" type of kiss from before; this kiss was our inner animals fighting for dominance. My back arched into him. His fingers dug into my thighs as he started moving me back and forth over his cock.

"I knew you'd growl," I confessed against his lips. I waited for another one. A growl that said he liked that I liked it, but instead I got something even better. His hand wrapped around me and flipped us on the couch. Sandwiched between the couch and his body, I was purring like a kitten. My fingers gripped his large biceps and dug in. His hips moved forward with hard pressure. I cried out. Our mouths devoured each other's and our body moved in sync, both of us spiraling towards the ultimate pleasure. I nipped at his bottom lip, spurring him to be even more aggressive.

Lord, I'd never had it rough, and now I didn't know if I would ever be able to go back to boring old "normal" sexual encounters. This thing between us was an undeniable attraction that made every touch colossal. His large hand moved around my waist and grasped my breast. His hand was so large on my B-cups that I felt a little pang of insecurity pop into my head. I squashed it down. If he wasn't into them, he wouldn't be paying so much attention to them. Squeezing, pinching my nipples through my bra.

I felt myself heading toward a fan-fucking-tastic orgasm.

"Jake!" I moaned and arched my back, needing to connect with him as much as I could. His body completely covered mine and his cock was creating hard but glorious friction between us. His mouth moved from my lips to my cheek, then my neck, and that brought me ten times closer.

"Jake, come in Jake." Somewhere in the house someone was calling through a walkie or something. No, NO!

"Please," I begged. He couldn't leave me like this, not when I was so close. I'd kill him! I'd feed him to his animals for a late night snack!

"Scream for me, sweetheart." He moved with such force that he buried me deep into the couch. His kisses on my neck grew more intense. I savored it. I was almost there.

Almost.

Right.

There.

Then he bit my neck and *growled*.

I exploded. Fucking hell, it was like a magic orgasm button on me. I screamed out, riding the pure, mind-bending waves of pleasure.

I collapsed against the couch, and his body was crushing me, but I didn't care. I liked it, actually.

"Perfection, sweetheart," he purred against me.

"Jake, come in Jake," the voice called again.

"Is it always like this?" I voiced.

"Yeah, this isn't a nine-to-five job; issues can arise at any time." He sat up and pulled my limp body up with him.

"Ok, well, have fun." I didn't know what else to say. I wasn't mad or anything. He looked at me, trying to figure out if I was upset or emotional that he had to leave. I guess for some women they wouldn't like that, but I was fiercely independent. Stuff like that wouldn't bother me unless I was just about to blow my load, so to speak.

"Really, this type of stuff doesn't bother me. Just don't leave me aching. Deal?" I thought it was a pretty good deal. He went on with his life as usual, and I got orgasms. This one-week bet was sounding better and better.

"Pure perfection, sweetheart." He leaned in to kiss me softly before untangling us and standing. His erection looked almost painful behind his jeans.

"I can take care of that for you. Remember, I'm a pro?" My fingers inched towards it.

"Rain check. Gotta work." He winked and strolled away towards the walkie. I heard him talking into it somewhere as I just relaxed back onto the couch and enjoyed my post-over-clothes-coital bliss.

I went to bed a few hours later. Jake still hadn't returned and honestly, that sucked for him. I wasn't lying when I said I was a bed hog. I knew that whenever he tried to get into bed he would be fighting off my star-fished body, which would be no easy feat.

A loud alarm woke me up from a nice dream.

"Rayne, I swear to God I'm going to break that alarm." I tried to roll over but couldn't. I was stuck. Panic arose in me and I woke up fully. I wiggled but nothing happened.

"Stop wiggling that ass against me, sweetheart." And I stopped moving. My eyes opened and I turned around to see a very cute, but very sleepy Jake.

I looked on the other side of the bed towards the alarm clock.

"5a.m.! No fucking way! I'm out." I tried to disentangle myself from him, but it seemed like he found a way to keep my bed-hogging problem at bay—by restraining me. He was wrapped around me like an octopus.

"Jake, I can't be up this early. I'm going to be a monster," I groaned. This was so not happening to me. I thought Rayne was bad by waking up at 6a.m.

His grip loosened and his hands started roaming. I felt his cock behind me start to grow hard.

"Seriously? No, you go to work. I'm going back to sleep." I closed my eyes, trying to do just that.

A hot mouth touched my bare neck, sending a bolt of electricity through my skin.

"I'll make the hours worth it." I scoffed, but boy did he ever.

An hour later, I was dressed in a pair of leggings tucked into a pair of fashion biker boots and a button up denim tunic, my hair was pulled back into a nice bun, with minimal makeup. Jake was, of course, looking fine in his signature Henley shirt, jeans, and boots, with a wee bit of scruff on his face that felt fabulous between my legs this morning.

We didn't have morning sex, because he said there wasn't enough time, which I rolled my eyes at. I mean, really. We could have had a quickie and been all set.

"Hop on." He sat on an ATV and patted the back for me. Ugh, this was so not my thing, but I did it anyway. I straddled the machine and hugged Jake around the waist tightly. I was scared I'd fall off.

"We won't be going fast; you don't have to hold on if you don't want to." I kept holding on. Last time I trusted a man around here, I almost lost a finger.

Chapter Ten

He started the four-wheeler and we began moving towards God knows where.

We passed a few habitats, and he explained to me which animals were there and how many. He promised I would get to know their names as the week went by. I was beginning to see how massive this rescue was, and we hadn't even covered a quarter of it.

"This is the front of the rescue. You passed through here when you came for the birthday party." He stopped in front of a block building. I recognized it from Natalie's birthday party, but to be honest, I wasn't truly paying attention to it last time. I think there was a gift shop in it. Oh, and they made us watch a movie on the dos and don'ts on the rescue, along with some other information

I'm sure was important. I hopped off the machine and Jake followed.

"I want you to see the rescue from the beginning to the end." He beamed and I shuffled behind him as he walked through the open double doors in the back of the building. It wasn't super large, maybe 1,000 square feet.

It had a desk, a ton of shirts, and other gift shop memorabilia with the Wild Rescue logo on it. I took it all in and wandered around, leaving Jake behind. I giggled at some of the stuffed animals with their big wide eyes and little T-shirts on. There was a lot of hippie-like stuff there. I guess "save the animals" in tie-dye did have a good draw.

I found my ovaries starting to ache when I looked at the cute onesies with animal-shaped heads on the front and a tail on the butt. Not wanting to go down that road, I moved on and saw a bunch of laminated papers displayed on a wall. You could adopt all sorts of animals, which was pretty much just sponsoring them. There were so many options, so many ways to help. I was starting to feel a little in awe of what all they had to do to help these animals. It wasn't like a circus or a place that wanted to just get a bunch of money off of having animals.

I turned back towards Jake to see him talking with an older woman who was working around the desk. Wanting to go say hello, I walked over and introduced myself.

"Hi, I'm Cammy, Jake's hostage for the week." I waved. I noticed Jake bite back a smile as I stopped at the desk.

"Hostage, interesting. I'm Patty, too old to be working but Jake just can't get rid of me." She was tall, and pretty thin. She looked like she was healthy, though. Her gray hair was cut short and she was wearing a blue polo shirt and khaki cargo shorts. I had seen a few other people wearing clothes like that so it must be their uniform.

"Nice to meet you. Jake here was just showing me around the rescue. Seems pretty snazzy so far." I looked around the little gift shop again.

"We do put in a ton of hours keeping this place nice. I'm glad my grandbabies have somewhere they can go to learn about animals, and not have to worry about a crack needle getting stuck in their foot." Her face told me she wasn't joking. I felt a little awkward after that comment.

"Yes, well, we can't have that happening." Thank God Jake decided to save me at that moment.

"I'm going to finish giving my hostage a tour of her prison. We'll see you later." He wrapped his arm around my waist and directed me towards the door. We hopped back onto the ATV and he showed me the pavilion where Natalie had her birthday party, which happened to be near another smaller barn with two goats, Francine and Frank, and a pig named Judice, hanging out behind the fence.

"You have quite the variety of animas here," I yelled at him.

"No need to shout, I can hear ya just fine." He turned down a path and we came to a block building with two girls coming out of it. Both girls were young, maybe twenty. One had long brown hair and was petite but had a nice rack, and the other girl had caramel colored hair, petite as well, but with no rack. I wondered what they did here. As soon as their eyes landed on Jake I understood why they were here. Both of them had a sultry look in their eyes. They wanted the man straddling the machine right now.

"Girls, I'd like you to meet Cammy. She'll be helping us on the rescue this week." Jake helped me off the ATV and then got off to stand next to me. The girls' eyes swung to me and I saw a little sneer on the blonde's face. I felt my inner bitch rear her head. These girls wanted to play high school mean girls? Fine, little did they know, I *owned* high school.

"Hiya, girls. Nice to meet you. What's your name?" I walked up and shook their hands. Showing them I was no little girl. I was a full bitch-blooded woman, if needed.

"I'm Autumn." The brown haired girl shook my hand but it was a weak shake. The blonde shook it next, a little firmer but still. Pansy.

"I'm Helen." We took a step back from each other and their eyes went straight back to Jake.

"Autumn and Helen run our social media sites. Keeping everything updated and reaching new people.

Social media has become one of our best tools for educating the public on exotic animal abuse, along with what we do here." You could tell this place was his love. And these girls were helping him share that love with the world. I guess I could let their little love glares roll off my shoulder. Autumn suddenly got really excited, and had something to say.

"Oh and it's time for another picture, Jake. Don't forget about it." I looked at him in confusion. He sighed, but nodded.

"A picture of me holding Casey got out onto Facebook and ever since then, I've been dubbed the Extremely Hot Animal Guy." He looked uncomfortable, like that name was something new. I mean honestly, I bet he's been called that many times before a picture went viral. Helen piped up with more on the subject.

"It's been great for the rescue, though. There have been articles written about him and his work. He's all over Instagram and Pinterest. Donations have been coming in to support him, along with more hits on our website. Sorry, Jake, but sex appeal sells. You've got it going on, and we are going to use it." While I didn't like the way she said it, I understood. And it was probably true. I had heard about a hot veterinarian a couple months back, and his practice was booming. I bet things were doing great now that the world saw the hot man behind the scenes.

"Yeah, yeah, maybe this weekend." He nudged me towards the building while saying goodbye to the girls.

"Bye!" I told them and they both stayed silent, watching us walk through the door. The room was open, it had a mini fridge, and a long shelf desk covering the wall. A man with a bald head turned in his computer chair. "Oh, Jake, you shouldn't have. My birthday isn't until next Monday." The man appeared to be in his late twenties, had a trimmed beard around his lips, and glasses. He was a large man, but not heavy. He reminded me of a teddy bear. I just wanted to hug him.

"Chip, I'd like you to meet Cammy. Cammy, meet Chip. He's our marketing expert and editor of the Wild Newsletter." I noticed he was designing something on the computer. Papers were scattered everywhere and the printer was doing its job as we spoke.

"Nice to meet you." I went to shake his hand and he pulled me in for a hug. While I wasn't always a hugger, I felt like this hug was okay.

"Cammy, nice to meet you. And if you ever get tired of this brute, then come talk to me." He winked and went to go grab something from a cabinet.

"We'll let you get back to work. Send me the weekend letter tonight. I'll look it over," Jake said and once again steered me back out toward the ATV. I felt I had been running around with him all day, seeing habitats and meeting his staff, but really, it had only been about two hours. The day was still young and I was somehow still awake.

After we climbed back onto the ATV, he took off and told me about a few more of the animals as we passed them. Each of the habitats had an indoor and outdoor area, with a customized environment that the animal would expect based on where it originated. We passed the wallaby area, and I kid you not, that little asshat Dundee gave me the death look. He wanted to finish the job of taking off my finger. I looked up at the Spanish moss-covered oak trees and marveled at how peaceful it was out here. Until I heard a loud roar.

My fingers gripped onto Jake's side a little harder.

"We're coming up on the larger habitats back here." Larger? Goodness, did he really have big lions, tigers, and bears back here? So far we had seen plenty of animals, but other than the horse and the wolves, nothing was huge.

We drove by tall fences that surrounded a couple acres of mostly fields. I saw a lion get swatted at by a lady lion. He backed away and lay down next to her. Maybe she had a headache.

There were a few other lady lions in there as well. I felt like I was in *The Lion King*.

"That's Talib and Subira. She's his number one. They were brought to us from a drug bust. The owners were using them as guard dogs for their drugs, giving them a status of power. They were chained and had maybe a fifteen-foot radius to move around in." He was calm telling me their story, but I could tell it made him unhappy. I looked at them now and they looked to be enjoying themselves. They had a big space to run around in, a little play area where they could climb on stuff and a small pool with giant balls scattered around the field. They were living a good life now. I felt myself snuggle in a little bit closer to Jake. What he did here was starting to pull at my heartstrings a little.

Chapter Eleven

Wild Rescue was home to twenty-six big cats, including lions, tigers, a liger, panthers, and two cheetahs. We also passed by the home of a big grizzly bear. For some reason, the bear was scarier to me than the big cats we saw. Jake told me a few of the stories of the animals we stopped to watch. One of the panthers was abused. The owner wanted a big cat, but then as it got bigger, he used to beat it on the head with a shovel. Then we saw a bear who was retired from the circus.

One of the tigers, named Nala, used to be drugged so that people could take pictures with her for money. I felt sick to my stomach when we came to a stop at a house that had a large pond behind it.

"I'm not a big lover of animals. However, I'm really glad you do what you do, Jake, and that you've found a way to give these poor babies a home." I wasn't a very emotional person. Truth be told, I've only cried twice in my adult life. Once when Rayne accidentally hit me in the nose. It hurt so bad, I swore it was broken. Thank goodness it wasn't. The other time was when my parents split up. I was upset because I thought everything was great, but apparently it wasn't. They were just growing in different directions. I still talk to both, and when we are all together, they get along nicely. My sister and I both had nice childhoods, and aren't bitter about it. But when I first heard they were splitting, I was sad. Then I moved on. Life was too short for a lot of tears and sadness. So the fact that on my first day with Jake and the animals I was close to crying, made me feel a little uneasy and out of my comfort zone.

"This is where our vet lives. Over to the right you can see the intern and employees' homes." He pointed to the right and I noticed a couple of houses. All different sizes. My guess was it was like a dorm type of situation, unless you had a family.

"Come on, I want you to meet the doctor." We walked into the house, and it was not what I was expecting. It looked like a doctor's office. I could see a big surgical room with a window to the right, and a wooden desk right before that.

Jake was kind of cute, how he wanted me to meet all the people that he worked with. I'll admit I was intrigued by the man and what went on in his life. I still said we were different, but I knew he had a wicked tongue and he cared deeply for this rescue.

"Hey, Doc, I want you to meet someone," my tour guide called out. I snickered at the thought. Jake was my little safari guide. Cute.

"Well, hello there. The young lady that was bitten by the wallaby!" The same older man who had tried to explain to me why Jake had his arm up a horse's ass walked into the room. He was tall, in decent shape, and had a trimmed white beard and gray hair. He looked to be in his sixties, but I wasn't the best at the age guessing game.

"That would be me." I flashed him my middle finger that was now bandage free.

"I'm Cammy." I waved. He smiled, then his green eyes looked at Jake with a different type of smile. Like an "I'm proud of you, son" type of smile.

"I'm just helping out for the week." I tried to put that out there. In no way was I staying here for good. Nope. Not happening.

"Cammy, I'm Doctor Nick. My wife, Hannah, is assisting Casey right now with her lunch, but you can meet her in a minute."

"Hannah!" a voice that sounded just like the doctor's screamed in the room. I looked to my left and saw a big birdcage with a large gray bird sitting on the top. He screamed again, and I felt a little creeped out that it sounded just like the doctor. I would hate to be here at night and have it start talking. Nightmares galore, right there.

"That's Booma, our African Grey. He has a very extensive vocabulary, and as you heard, can imitate tones of voice." The doctor walked over to the bird and scratched its neck. The bird obviously liked it, but I was still leery. That beak looked sharp. Everything on this rescue could bite me or kill me. I eased over closer to Jake, ready to take cover should it fly over and attack me.

"He won't hurt you," Jake whispered to me, and I stuck my tongue out at him.

"He's an animal, they all bite," I countered, using his own words against him. He didn't say anything, but his eyes skimmed over me, then came back up to meet mine, desire burning in those blue pools. He wanted to bite me. I felt my cheeks blush a little, because to be honest, I wanted him to. My mind had started thinking about all the wicked things I wanted to do to him, when a woman entered the room, carrying a little tiger in her arms.

"Casey is eating better; she drank the whole bottle in a snap. Oh, hi, Jake!" She had really curly black hair and deep brown eyes. She was in decent shape, but then considering the load she was carrying, I could see how she looked good.

"Give me my girl." Jake walked over to her and lifted the little orange tiger right out of her arms. Did tigers purr? Because I'm pretty sure I heard it purr as it snuggled in his arms.

"I'm Hannah, Nick's wife and other vet on the premises. We help take care of all the animals when they need us." She smiled and rubbed the tiger's head.

"Cammy, Jake's hostage for the week." I smiled, then went to peek at the kitty in Jake's arms. I was curious about the mysterious Casey.

Now, maybe it was my maternal clock ticking away, or maybe it was like what happened with Jacob imprinting on Renesmee in *Twilight*, but when I looked into that little tiger's eyes, something in me clicked. I wanted to care for that little cub. I wanted her to grow into a big tiger and be happy.

"Hi, baby. Oh, you are such a pretty girl," I cooed at the cub. I walked over and for the first time in my life, I wasn't afraid that an animal was going to bite my fingers off. I knew she could eat me, even at her size, if she wanted to, but I was oddly unconcerned.

Her big, blue eyes were watching me as she brought her paws up to bat Jake's face playfully.

Be still my heart.

"Yes, you are going to grow up and be a bad ass tiger, aren't you?" Something had to have possessed me. I was baby talking to a tiger. I reached out and her paws touched my hand. I felt claws, but not in a bad way. She was batting my fingers.

"She likes you." Jake's voice was husky. My hand moved back to my side and my eyes flew up to his. He was looking at me with even more hunger in his gaze. Oh hell.

"I like her too," I admitted. I heard a growl from the man consuming my thoughts and looked down at the tiger. I didn't want to embarrass myself by jumping on him in front of the doctors. Swiftly Jake walked towards Hannah and handed Casey back to her. I may have heard the little tiger meow *nooo*, but that could have been in my head.

"I've got more to show Cammy; I'll be back later for Casey. It's my week." I barely had time to say goodbye before Jake was dragging my ass back out to the ATV.

"I wasn't done talking to them, you brute!" I took a step back but was lifted up and placed on the machine in seconds. *Holy strong arms, Batman!* Instead of Jake sitting in front of me, this time he was behind me, his chest against my back. His surprisingly hard cock was pressed against my lower back. A little shiver coursed through me. I wanted that cock.

My head fell back a little and my eyes closed, my thoughts solely on getting pleasured by the man behind me. I felt like a cat in heat around him; all I wanted to do was lift my ass in the air and wave it around like *come and get me big boy*! I thought I felt his chest rumble behind me, but he also had just turned on the four wheeler.

My back pressed against his torso even more since he was speeding us somewhere. I mentally crossed my fingers that we were heading back to the lodge for some naughty time, but instead he drove off the beaten path and into the woods. My mouth pursed in confusion. Uh, did he take me for a woodsy type of girl?

Chapter Twelve

We passed by a shed with doors and he parked us to the side of it. We were completely alone. Hmmm, maybe being out in the woods wasn't such a bad thing after all right now. The ATV was still rumbling, and I won't lie, feeling horny, combined with the subtle vibrations of the machine between my legs, was making me feel extra frisky. When I started to turn so I could figure out what he had planned, Jake turned off my vibrations. I pouted a little at that but decided we could play another time this week on the ATV.

"It's very quiet out here," I commented, looking around. I wondered what was in the shed. I kinda noticed two dirt lines that went through the trees like a path. Maybe from a car or truck?

"Jake?" He hadn't said a word. My body turned back towards his and he looked pained.

"Jake?" Should I shake him or something? I got up onto my knees and faced him. He was looking off in the trees, but switched his attention to me now that I was facing him. Staring into his blue eyes made me want to kiss him again. And even though we already had our first kiss, I had a feeling that more kisses from Jake would feel like a first kiss every time. Free falling into his blissful touch. He didn't make me wait for it. He knew exactly what I wanted.

His fingers wrapped lightly around the back of my neck and pulled me down to him. He was assertive in his kiss, taking control, while giving me what I craved. My fingers gripped the tops of his shoulders, wanting to be closer. His other hand went to my hip and pushed me so I clashed with his body. Oh, heck yeah. I straddled his hips and ground down on him a little. I was a tease, but to be honest, I just straight up wanted him. Sex on one of these things could be interesting.

"Plans have changed, not fucking you yet," he stated as I moved over that big piece of man meat. Those blasphemous words stopped me mid-grind. I tried to pull back to question what the hell he just said, but he lifted me off him, swung off the ATV and laid me down on the seat cushion.

"What the hell do you mean, *plans have changed?* I want sex." I lifted my head to look at him just as he nipped my clit through my leggings. A yelp flew from my chest. He nuzzled my sex and I was starting to forget what I was saying. Something about plans?

"You aren't ready to talk about it yet. We'll wait until you get more accustomed to this." His fingers gripped the waistband to my leggings and started pulling them down. Even though I was confused by his words, I lifted my hips so he could get them down to the tops of my boots. I was bare and on display for all the woodland creatures to see, but I wasn't shy. Jake was looking at me like he was going to devour the shit out of my pussy and I was salivating with anticipation for him to do it. I didn't wait long.

He latched on and I moaned as he licked, sucked, and paid special attention to that little bundle of nerves that was driving me wild. My fingers gripped the handle bars above my head, anything to tether myself to this ATV and what the tongue between my legs was doing to me. He lapped at my core with force. He was out to prove something. What? I did not fucking care at the moment. My body tensed, my hips lifted in sync with his tongue. I felt so close.

"Please, Jake," I begged. I needed this release like I needed to breathe. A finger entered me, and my back bowed.

"Holy fuck!" I cried out. His finger moved in and out, curling right at my sweet spot. My vision blurred and my body froze up and then exploded. Like screaming-louder-than-the-damn-lions-roar-in-the-fields type of exploded. Jake's hand gripped my waist, keeping me pinned to his mouth.

"Jake, come in Jake. We've got a problem." And the good feeling I had just been graced with vanished. Problem? What problem? Jake untangled himself from my legs and grabbed his walkie.

"Jake here." He looked me over; a little gloss from my wetness coated his lips. He noticed me looking and licked his lips clean. Did I just orgasm again? Maybe...

"Juno snuck out."

"Shit," he cursed, while turning a knob on his walkie.

"Attention, we have a code red. Find the nearest indoor enclosure and wait until I say it's over." Then he switched the knob again.

"Derek. Get the tranquilizer." I pulled my leggings up faster that you can say freak out. Which I was doing, a little.

"Who snuck out?" I asked as I sat up on the ATV and Jake sat in front of me.

"Juno, a twenty-eight-month-old lion cub. She is mostly harmless, but could still kill someone if she wanted to." And there it was. I kept thinking all the animals were going to get out and eat me and it was now a possibility. Instead of panicking like I wanted to, I just held onto Jake's waist as he sped off toward the big cat that was on the loose.

Derek was waiting by the lodge with a large gun. Oh shit.

"She's around the porch. Probably wanting one of the goats," Derek said, as Jake jumped off the ATV and grabbed the gun.

"Stay with Cammy." He pointed to Derek with a fierce look. Jake slowly started walking around the porch, probably so his boots wouldn't make noise on the wood. Could one really sneak up on a lion though? I wasn't so sure that I wanted to stay here anymore. I mean, if lions were going to be getting loose and running around, I would probably get eaten. I wasn't very fast, or graceful. One stumble and I'd be kitty food in a heartbeat. My armpits started to sweat from nerves as Jake got closer and closer to the corner of the house.

"Come on, sweetheart." Derek's voice brought me out of my panicked state. He was holding his large calloused hand out to me. I was confused.

"You'll see; you don't want to miss this." I was still confused as hell but I grabbed the man's hand and he led me, very quickly, to the back of the house where there were a bunch of people.

Waiting for Jake.

Waiting for Jake to come around the corner with his tranquilizer gun for a lion, that, from the looks of the cake and balloons, was just a ploy to get him over here.

A few thoughts drifted through my mind as Jake came around the corner, gun up and ready to fire. Everyone yelled *happy birthday*!

While I thought it was cool that they wanted to throw him a surprise birthday party, I had just come on the man's lips. Couldn't they have waited like, half an hour?

Jake dropped the gun and a smile broke out on his face. His eyes went to Derek's, and I could tell he wanted to throttle the flannel-wearing man. His eyes moved to me next and I mouthed happy birthday. Maybe I would give him a birthday blow job or something of the sort. Ever since I saw his dick yesterday in the shower, I had been wanting to get my hands on it. While everyone stopped Jake to say hello, I noticed that he was not shaking hands with anyone. Which in turn made me giggle a little, thinking of where that hand had been not too long ago. It was like a dirty little secret between us.

"Enjoy your toys?" Derek asked, shoulder bumping me. Because he was larger than me, I stumbled a little. I was about to answer when I spotted a little fluffy creature rolling in the grass by Hannah.

"Yep, be right back." My eyes were glued to the little baby tiger having fun with some small toy.

"Cammy, nice to see you again." Hannah's sweet voice called out to me.
"Yes! It feels like it's been so long," I joked, then went down on my knees by the little cub.

"She is adorable." I wanted to pet her but realized that I knew nothing about baby tigers. I doubted that they were like sweet little kittens that would curl up on your lap while you petted them.

"That she is. She's our little trooper." Hannah smiled at the cub and took a sip out of her red Solo cup.

"What's her story? Every animal here has one, or so I'm learning." I sat there as Hannah told me Casey's story. A man was looking to make some money, so he travelled around the U.S. to festivals or big parties, and accepted cash in exchange for people having their picture made with a tiger cub. They could pet her, handle her how they pleased, and pose for the camera. He made a lot, sadly. Poor little Casey had been ripped away from her mother and thrown into the world of "cub petting," as I learned that it was actually called that. He fed her, and housed her, but not like he should have. She got sick because she was like a newborn and had no real immune system yet. Thankfully, before he could sell her off, kill her, or God knows what else, the State stepped in and she was brought to the rescue. Hannah, her husband, and Jake took personal care of her, alternating weeks because she still required nighttime feedings. She was eleven months old and soon would be big enough that she wouldn't need milk anymore. They've only had her for four weeks now and she was happy and at home.

"But she has gotten sick once since she's been here. When that happens we have to monitor her closely so she doesn't get worse." Hannah ended her story. Poor baby Casey.

"I know this sounds stupid to say, but does she bite you?" I had to know.

"Oh, yes. She used to not know how her teeth would hurt, but she has learned to be gentle." She demonstrated by putting her hand in the tiger's mouth, which she opened for but didn't try and take her fingers off. Interesting.

The tiger yawned, and laid across Hannah's feet and relaxed. Sleep was probably going to overtake her soon.

"So, Cammy, what brings you here to help out at a place like this?" Hannah asked nicely. The only reason I was here was because I lost a bet to Jake, instead of helping for the cause of the animals, which made me sort of feel bad. But I was not one to regret anything, so I told her the truth.

"Jake and I made a bet, he won, and I'm here for the week. Not sure what help I will be; as you can probably tell, I'm not a hard labor type of girl. But I'm always up to try new things." It was the best answer I could give. I looked around and saw Jake looking at me. His blue eyes melted another layer I had built up against him. He did so much. Everyone around him was smiling and having a great time.

"He's a good man. Needs to settle down, though." Subtle much? I looked back at Hannah to see her watching me watching Jake. Unsure of what else to say, I stood up.

"He's all right." I winked and strode off toward the man of the hour.

"Happy birthday. I didn't know I was getting the honor of being in your presence on your birthday. I am so humbled," I teased. The two people that were talking to him struck up a conversation between themselves so it was like Jake and I were alone.

"Best birthday gift a man could ask for," he uttered as he stuck his finger in his mouth. Oh God.

I felt like Oprah, handing out gifts to everyone. You get an orgasm, you get an orgasm, everyone gets an orgasm! Mini-orgasms were happening everywhere just by him sucking the remnants of my wetness off his damn fingers.

"Maybe if you convince me, you'll get an even better birthday gift." I pressed my tongue to the side of my cheek, hinting at a blowjob. His eyes narrowed at my cheek and took a step closer.

"A better gift would be stripping you down with my teeth, your hands gripping the full-length mirror in the guest room, while I palm that sweet ass and feed your tight pussy my cock…inch by inch until you are so full you are up on your toes to accommodate me." I wanted to hold onto his body because I felt like my knees were going to give out.

"Definitely sounds better," I whimpered, need strangling my throat. Never in my thirty years had I ever been on fire like this. He lit me up and kept me burning for him. It was something I could easily get addicted to, whether I wanted that or not.

"But it won't be this birthday." He pulled back with a smug smile. Was he enjoying riling me up like this, then letting me sit on it? And not sit on it in a *good* way.

"What is your deal? I gave in; I'm willing to let you have your wicked way with me. I'm here. What do you want?" I whisper-raged, totally up in his face. Thank God no one was paying attention to us, because I was sure this looked a little heated.

"What I want, you aren't ready to hear yet. So relax, sweetheart. Enjoy the ride. I promise you there will be one….just not today." He leaned in and pressed a sweet kiss to my cheek before walking away, as if he didn't just get me all hot and bothered, then throw some Arson-like shit on me. Arson.

Rayne! I needed to talk to Rayne.

Chapter Thirteen

Without bringing attention to myself, I moved with haste up the stairs and stepped into the house. My phone was up on the nightstand, so I quickly ran up the stairs and swiped it to life.

I had a few texts from my salon; everything was good. Mary loved me. They were surviving.

I called Rayne as soon as I finished sending back the salon a thumbs up.

She answered quickly.

"Helloo there!"

"Rayne. Jake is pulling an Arson. I repeat— Jake is pulling an Arson. What do I do?" It was like déjà vu all over again.

"I knew it. What is he saying? *I'm what you deserve, baby? You're not ready yet? I want to see you pregnant and getting round with my child inside you?*" She lowered her voice at the last bit, mocking her lover.

"Gah! He already pulled the first one with *I'm your alpha; I know what you need* speech. Now he just pulled the *you're not ready yet* part. What the hell am I gonna do? I don't want this life. I came here and I think a small part of me knew we would have fun, but that's what you thought with Arson and he was in love with you and wanted you to be his forever. Rayneeee." I had officially gone from mildly annoyed and horny to freaking out.

"Why don't you want that life?" she asked honestly. I rolled my eyes.

"Come on. I am not the type of girl that likes to get dirty. I mean, what they do here is really awesome. I saw all the animals today, and there is the cutest baby tiger that I'm going to mother the rest of the week. But it's just like a weird vacation. I'm all make-up, hair, and my salon. Jake is really hot, and he is realllly good with his tongue. But I don't think we could be around each other for any real length of time." Even as the words came out of my mouth, my mind was screaming it was a lie.

"I don't know, Cammy. Things and wants change. I wanted a guy, but I didn't think I would get a real alpha man like Arson. I also didn't really know if I wanted kids and here I am, knocked up, eating Fruit Loops because that's all this kid has been craving today. Maybe it's worth a shot." I mulled over her words. I hadn't told her yet that I wanted a family. She probably still thought I was living the single life, screwing with a bunch of hot guys. Maybe it was a stupid thought, but I didn't want her to think I was trying to take away her thunder. I hated to think that.

"Ok, I've got to go, but tell Cammy Jr. I love her!"

"Run all you want, but take it from me—love will catch you and knock you on your ass. Talk to you later."

We parted with those sweet words of hers.

Love. Pshhh. That was definitely not happening. I sat on the bed and looked around the room. I was a straight shooter, usually. But here I was, freaking out over something that could be nothing. I wasn't ready to open up to anyone yet about my new want of a family, so that was my secret for now. I stood up, feeling like Xenia on the verge of kicking some ass. If Jake thought he was going to lead me around, then he had another think coming.

I was Cammy Freaking Jennings; I once switched my bestie's toothpaste with lube. I was a force to be reckoned with.

I marched myself right back out to the backyard, where pretty much everyone had cleared out and gone back to their work. Only Derek, Tweedle Dee and Tweedle Dumb aka Autumn and Helen, and Jake, were chatting.

"Ok, get. Scoot, skiddaddle!" I shoo'd them away.

"Excuse us; we were just talking about something important," Autumn foolishly opened her mouth. Poor child, I know she didn't understand the predicament she was in. I mean, I know I looked like a sweet, redheaded cupcake on the outside, but I was a cherry bomb on the inside. Deciding to nip this whole thing in the bud, I walked right up to Jake and laid claim to his lips right in their faces.

Yep. Cammy Jennings was metaphorically peeing on Jake Wild.

I gripped his shirt, keeping him right in my grasp. I could practically hear the rolling of their eyes, but as long as I was getting the point across, I didn't care.

Jake had a grin on his face as I blew his mind, obviously enjoying my cavewoman maneuvers. When I pulled back, I looked at the girls with a little headshake and raised brow. My attitude pretty much said, *what? You wanna roll now? Bring it, bitches!* Both girls rolled their eyes but walked away. I turned to Derek to see him silently cracking up. His hands raised in a surrender position when he met my glare.

"I'll see you two around. Good luck, Jake." He laughed and walked away backwards, afraid to put his back to me. Yeah, I was a bad ass. I turned back to Jake, who had the biggest grin on his face. I felt like such a hurricane to the other people, but seeing his grin made me feel like a thunderstorm—soothing to some people on a warm summer day.

"Okay, listen here, Mr. Alpha Animal Man. You don't know me that well, so I'm going to impart some wisdom on you." I pointed my finger for emphasis. Which he unfortunately gripped, and pulled me up against his body.

I was a flailer when I got hyped up like this.

But this close to him, I couldn't flail. I felt like a cat in the bathtub. My inner cherry bomb was being doused, which fizzled my whole spiel.

"I can't let you have it when you're holding me!" I honestly felt like he just wrapped me in a calming blanket. No one could be angry when they were being held like this. Dammit!

Hearing my words, his damn smile just got bigger!

"I'm curious. I'll let you do your thing." He let me go, then went to sit on the wooden step, ready for what I was going to do.

"Well, you've ruined most of it. So you won't get the full Cammy effect now." I mean, honestly. I was deflated now. He messed with my mojo.

"Would it help if you pissed on my leg again?" A blush grew on my face, but I was starting to feel feisty again. His banter was working.

"Those children needed to be put in their place." I did the little attitude head shake. I was getting back into my flow.

"I didn't mind." He relaxed back, his body stretched out on those steps. Why did he look so hot just sitting there?

"Cammy." My attention that was roaming his body moved up to his face.

"Focus, you were about to lay it on me. Thick, I believe." Fuck, he was right. I needed to get it together.

"Damn straight. Wisdom. I'm not sure if you've noticed yet, but I am an interesting bird. I'm dramatic. I don't take shit from people, and I am a blunt girl. So this whole *you're not ready yet* thing isn't going to work for me. You have something to say, you say it. I don't have to like it, but I want the same thing from you. Give it to me straight. Ain't nobody got time to worry about what's going on in your head." That spiel was shorter than what I was thinking in my head. No dramatic flair. He really did deflate me!

"One hour." Huh?

"One hour what?" I was confused.

"I figured it would only take you one hour to come at me about that." He pointed to the clock that was on the house by the door behind him.

"You knew I would say something?" What was happening here? This was not going how I imagined. My arms crossed over my chest.

"I knew the moment we met that you were going to be a handful. I wouldn't expect anything less." Well, damn. That statement, in its own way, was kind of sweet.

"You're okay with that? My brand of crazy?" I could occasionally be a little much for some people. I had to keep my freak flag folded up during some interactions with people. Rayne got it. That's why she was my best friend. But the other men I've dated tried to rein me in. Impossible.

"It definitely keeps things interesting." He stood and wrapped his arms around me again. This time I didn't put up a fight.

"I was trying to be nice and not rush you. But I want to be straight with you, so you'll continue to be straight with me." I looked into his eyes as he spoke. This moment was going to be something. I just knew it.

"I knew you were more than a quick fuck. When the alpha in me saw the alpha in you, he saw his mate. The second half of his soul. His equal. Seeing you in my bed, in my home, around my animals, I'm not just fighting to keep your body. I'm fighting to win your heart. To prove that I am the man you need. Your forever."

BOOM.HEADSHOT. There it was. There it fucking was.

Chapter Fourteen

"I'm not sure this life is what I need," I admitted to him softly. It was honest. Jake seemed to be a great guy but I wasn't sure he was THE guy for me. But the real question I needed to ask myself was, could I wait and see? Maybe he was, and all I had to do was give it a real chance.

"I've got a week. We'll see what happens."

"Ok, I'll give it a shot." I should be open to the opportunity of something big. This felt like it had the makings for that. Something great.

"I think we should try that whole claiming thing over again. I need your scent on me more," he teased and I started giggling. Crisis averted, for now.

"As long as you aren't going to hold back the D from me." I narrowed my eyes at him. Withholding the D was going to be a deal breaker for me.

"My sweetheart wants the D?" he leaned down and purred against my lips.

"No, she needs it." I kissed him and damn, did his sexy lips take over and demand I give into him. The kiss only lasted a few seconds but I sure as hell would be feeling his lips on me the rest of the day.

"Let's get some lunch. Then it's time to get you to work." He winked as he walked with me, hand-in-hand, to make some sandwiches in the kitchen.

Lunch was uneventful. I was actually pretty damn hungry, so we both mauled our food silently. After I went to the bathroom to freshen up my face and hair a little, we got back on the ATV and went to the kitchen. And by kitchen, he wasn't talking about the kitchen at the house. He meant the kitchen where all the animals' food was prepared.

"Oh good Lord, no." I tried to walk right back out the door we'd just come in, but Jake just wheeled me back around.

"You seriously can't expect me to touch anything in this room. Nope. I can't." There was bloody meat everywhere.

Not really, but that's what it felt like. The area was chilled and clean, with lots of counters everywhere. There was a person placing chicken legs into a bucket; we exchanged hellos, but then they went back to their work. I also saw a chart with the words *whole rabbits* and *rats* written on it. I knew that some of the animals ate meat and they ate it raw, but I just preferred not to think of it. I loved to eat meat. But in my head, it just came naturally at the grocery store, packaged in foam trays and plastic wrap. Not slaughtered and cut up!

"I'm going to vomit." I hacked a little but I wasn't really going to blow chunks everywhere.

"What if I offer you an incentive plan this week? For each thing you do that is gross, I will owe you an earth-shattering orgasm. Deal?" I looked at him in disgust. How could he tease me with orgasms like this? Do dirty and gross things receive an orgasm. Was I a big enough slut that I could be bought with orgasms?

"Deal."

Yes, yes I was.

Despite him probably wanting to laugh hysterically, Jake just gave me a sexy smile and walked over to a large deep freezer to open it. He pulled out a bag with a dead rabbit inside.

"Nothing less than earth-shattering orgasms, or I feed you to a tiger, capisce?"

"Understood." He nodded me over. Gross. I walked over to where he was and looked in the freezer. Dead woodland creatures, and a shit-ton of meat. Thankfully, it looked like it came from the grocery store and not road kill.

"Twice a week the cats get whole prey. Don't make that face. They were humanely killed and we get them from a very reputable supplier." Still gross.

"Koda, the bear, gets fish, fruits, nuts, mice, and some berries. In the fridge is a ton of veggies and fruits along with milk creations for the babies, like Casey. And the meat mixtures for the cats, depending on the size. Every day there are interns, and employees go on their assigned routes and tend to the animals in the morning. Some animals get fed a couple times a day. For the wolves we stick to twenty pounds of meat per wolf." Goodness, this was a lot of information. I felt like I should be writing this down or something.

"We won't be feeding anything today. I have something else in mind to pop your rescue cherry."

Famous last words before I rubbed him in hand lotion and fed him to the wallaby.

There lies Jake, the man that died at the hands of his creatures, after making his very beautiful redheaded-lover scoop shit.

After we spent time in the kitchen we walked over to the habitats to clean.

I was currently cleaning shit.

I was going to need at least five orgasms to make up for what he was making me do.

Cleaning the cat cages. He was at home doing this dirty work. Raking, cleaning out their habitat, scooping up some poo to toss in a bag that was in a bucket. But I, on the other hand, hated cleaning my own apartment, let alone this. Alas, I was no quitter, so I ventured on. It was interesting to learn that each habitat fence had a few guillotine doors, one led to an indoor and outdoor feeding and sleeping area, the other was a part of a maze that led to different play areas depending on the animal. The bigger animals had big concrete enclosures that they call home sometimes as well.

My arms were getting kind of tired from the work we had been doing for a few hours, and I might have gotten a little sunburned. I wasn't sure what I expected, but being tired, sweaty, and dirty was what I should have thought would happen to me. We did manual labor until dinnertime—mostly cleaning, and preparing enrichment toys for tomorrow.

I was somewhat excited to watch the animals play with my little creations. At least I had something to look forward to tomorrow. Jake made us hamburgers and fries for dinner and I was so hungry I felt like one of the damn beasts outside. I made a mental note to shove a snack bar in my pants every couple of hours.

"I've got to go take care of a few more things. Go take a shower and relax. I'll be back soon." Jake leaned in and kissed my forehead. It was such an intimate gesture that I felt deep inside my chest. It was strange having someone show their feelings to you while you resisted soaking it in. I wasn't willing to give into any emotions right now. Sexual stuff I could do. But emotions? I wasn't ready for that.

"Okay. I'm pretty beat. I haven't worked this hard since Rayne made me go to one of her aerial yoga classes." That was something I would never do again. God, the woman did it pregnant, for Christ's sake, and I was like a bug tangled in a web.

"You did yoga?" His eyebrow went up, questioning me. I shrugged.

"I know it's good for you, but I just wanted to breathe and get a smoothie afterwards. Not sweat! It's hard! If I wanted to sweat that much, I'd go have sex." Except, I hadn't been with many guys that have made me sweat like that. Which brought me back to thinking about sex with Jake.

"Can we fuck like wild monkeys tonight?" What? It was a fair question.

"You look pretty beat; we will see when I get back." He opened the door and smiled at me. Jerk.

"Maybe I'll just love myself a little, then go to bed. How do you like them apples?" I did my head shake with attitude.

"That's my girl. Warm her up for me a little." He winked and walked out the door. I scoffed. I didn't need to warm my vagina up. She was already a freaking sauna down there. Deciding a shower sounded amazing, I walked up the stairs, discarded my dirty clothes and hopped in. It was pure heaven. God, I ached. He needed to get a massage therapist on staff here. I bet everyone would appreciate that.

After my shower, I grabbed one of his T-shirts and put on a pair of cute, light blue shorts, then went back downstairs to rest on the couch.

Chapter Fifteen

Apparently, I was beat, because I passed out on the couch and didn't wake up until the morning. At 6a.m., with Jake wrapped around me in his bed.

"I hate your alarm," I grumbled and tried to roll over, but Jake's steel-like arms kept me against his body.

"Wake up, sweetheart." I groaned at his hot, sleepy voice.

"I'll marry you. Just let me sleep in every day." I was grasping at straws and feeling his body silently shaking with laughter behind me, I knew I had lost this battle.

"Deal." He laughed and I untangled myself from him in a huff of frustration. I wasn't marrying him and he called my bluff. I stormed off into the bathroom to do my business and when I was done he was up and putting on his shirt.

"We didn't have sex last night." I pouted; I was really looking forward to it.

"You mean you don't remember?" He turned to me and looked dead serious. Oh shit. I was pretty tired, but I don't remember getting from the couch to the bed. I wiggled a little bit to see if I was sore at all and came back with nothing. Asshole. If we had sex, my lady bits would have been deliciously sore from that giant slinging hammer he had between his legs.

"I do, I'm just trying to forget. Hoping it was just beginners' nerves. Next time should be better. Maybe you.." And he was on me, pinning me to the bed.

"Surprisingly, when you run your mouth like that it turns me on to no end." He kissed me and pressed that hammer against my thigh. I lifted my hips toward it like a magnet. God, I really was turning into a horny alley cat around him. In the blink of an eye, I reached my hand down underneath his waistband and wrapped my hand around his cock.

The world would try to collapse around us, but I was going to touch him, dammit!

His body shuddered a little and that spurred me on even more. I needed to touch, taste, and please him. I wanted those growls. I wanted to know what noises he made when he came. In a hurry, I pushed down the boxers he wore to sleep and released him. He was so hard, and yet silky smooth at the same time.

I felt so at ease touching him. It was like destiny. His penis literally belonged in my hands. Pulling my lips from his, I mumbled for him to roll over, which he did, but took me with him. I liked that he was so strong. I'd never been with a guy that could maneuver me like that; it was hot.

There was no need for words between us. Despite not knowing each other's middle names, he knew so much about me. My character. He knew exactly what I wanted and what I was going to do. I had a reputation to uphold, after all—sucking dick like a pro.

"Shirt. Off," I demanded. I was going to taste every single muscle of his torso. No ab left behind, my new motto. Why was he even wearing a shirt to begin with? He shucked off his shirt and laid back down as I sat up to eye fuck him. He really was something. All that hard labor has done his body good. I bet he doesn't even need to go to the gym.

When our eyes connected I felt something stir inside me. This man was something different. Something strong and undeniable. Not wanting to think about anything else, especially his feelings or what this could be, I got to work on my new motto. A soft growl bubbled up from his chest at the first contact of my lips to his warm skin. Hell, I groaned a little. His body was pure sin, my soon to be addiction. I nibbled, sucked, licked every part I could, down to the part of him I had been dying to have some one on one time with.

My eyes said hello to his cock and I gently wrapped the length of him with my hand, running teasing strokes up and down. I brought my lips to the tip and proceeded to rub it against my lips like I was putting on lipstick. A small bead of precum coated my lips, making me lick it off. I moaned at the taste. Salty mixed with Jake Wild.

"Suck my cock, sweetheart. Let your alpha out to play." His demand struck at my need to please him, and even his little alpha animal analogies that he kept making were starting to make me hot. I was a fucking alpha bitch. I could handle this man like I owned every part of him, because right now I did. The crazy cavewoman came out after thinking like that. I gripped him and growled *mine* against him before shoving my mouth over his silky head. I didn't relent. I wanted him begging me. Gripping me. Growling at me.

His hands went to my hair and his hips thrust upward, meeting me with every bob of my head. Thrilled with his reaction, I swirled my tongue, sucked faster, then switched directions of my head. I sat up and quickly moved between his legs. I wanted to get lost in his eyes as he came down my throat. The sight before me made me almost come. His tensed abs, the neck muscles slightly strained, parted lips, and labored breaths. I fucking owned this man.

His blue eyes met with mine and together we watched as he melted beneath my touch. My mouth hugged his engorged member, along with my hand for what my lips couldn't touch. I pleasured him in sync until his jaw fell slack, stomach tensed, hips thrust upwards, and that growl I wanted came from his parted lips, then turned into a groan. I sucked down his release and never took my eyes off his. Watching him orgasm was an aphrodisiac. I wanted to do it again and again. Rayne's mother, the sex therapist, always told me the man you are meant to be with is the man who you not only want to give a blowjob to, but you craved it.

I craved Jake. Feeling the need to escape my thoughts, I sat up and blurted out something random.

"What's your middle name?"

He shook his head and curled his finger for me to come closer. Even though I was feeling vulnerable, I crawled up to him.

"You know that you can keep fighting it, but I'm not giving up, right?" I knew this, so I nodded. I was starting to lose my mind in this whole ordeal.

"Cole. What's yours?"

"Jake Cole Wild. Simple. Mine is Renee. Cammy Renee Jennings." I liked my name as a whole. My parents did well in choosing my given name.

"Perfect," he purred and pulled me in for a kiss.

"Uh, don't you want me to brush my teeth or something first?" Not that I made it a habit of swallowing, but the ones I had did not want to taste their own love juice on my tongue. His answer was to kiss the doubts right out of me. Jake was not a weak man. He was exactly what he had been telling me, an alpha. And this alpha couldn't have given two shits about me having a dirty mouth; in fact, he was devouring that mouth with a passion.

When his hand started to creep towards my sweetness, I did something I never thought I would ever do.

"Rain check? I'm feeling pretty powerful right now. Let me have this moment, okay?" I was turning down an orgasm.

I pulled back to look at him and saw a look on his face that I couldn't figure out.

"You can make it up to me throughout the day if you really feel like it." I kissed him on the lips with a big smack and hopped off the bed. Feeling revitalized, I got to work on my beautification process for the day. Even though I knew it would probably be ruined, I was still not going to do this without a fight.

Chapter Sixteen

Both of us fully dressed and ready for the day, I grabbed a pop tart out of his pantry and we headed towards the dead animal kitchen. After putting on some thick gloves, I helped Jake and a few of the other workers put together the buckets of meat. After we put together – no joke– like a thousand pounds of meat, I was starting to wonder how the hell they paid for all of this. Donations? Gifts? This rescue was probably a huge money-sucker.

The business woman in me wanted to have a look at everything and figure out the numbers. I was pretty good with numbers, and my business had been successful since I started it at age twenty-three.

"So much meat," I groaned as I helped put the buckets into the carts that the interns and employees pulled to all of the cages. Another round of people grabbed their buckets for cleaning and grabbing poop. Every person who worked there was wearing a shirt with Wild Rescue on the front, but there were three colors: white, green, and blue. I asked one of the men who was wearing a green shirt, and he said the color indicated what level of employee they were. Green shirts took care of the big animals. Blue the level under that, and so on. Interesting concept, but it looked like it worked.

I also helped gather all of the enrichment toys that I helped make and was excited to follow behind one of the interns to watch one of the creatures play with it.

I laughed as one of the bobcats pounced and played with my little toilet paper roll with treats stuffed inside of it. Jake had small rats in his rolls, but I wasn't going that far. Sorry, bobcats.

When lunch rolled around, I went to check my phone while Jake made us something yummy, and cursed at my text notifications.

"Shit. Oh shit, shit, shit."

Rayne had sent me a message, asking if I was still coming over tomorrow to help her get ready for the Gala at the local Aquarium. A gala that I was supposed to attend. Crap, how had I forgotten about that? I had gotten so wrapped up in this whole Jake Wild adventure that I completely blanked on this event. Not that I had to do anything other than show my face around, but it was good for me to rub elbows with other business owners of Sarasota's elite.

Arson's gym had been a huge success, so naturally he was invited to go as well, and of course he would be bringing Rayne with him. The Gala was just a special night for the elites to kiss each other's asses, but in the end it couldn't hurt to make friends. There weren't too many pricks that could cause trouble, but if they happened to be a prick to you, having the right people on your team made a big difference.

"Everything okay?" Jake crossed his legs and arms across his chest on the door jam.

"No, I totally forgot I have a Gala I have to go to tomorrow night." Everything I needed was at home. My dress, which thankfully I had ordered a month ago, was hanging sweetly in my closet, ready to go. All of my makeup. Christ, I needed to get a pedicure and manicure to match it; I was still wearing the red polish from the bet, and my dress was definitely not red.

"The Sarasota Elites Gala?" he questioned.

"Yeah, how did you know?" His answer rather surprised me.

"I was invited, never gave them an answer. You need to go?" He uncrossed his arms but ran a hand through his hair.

"Yeah, it's always good to go to make or keep connections. Plus, Rayne will be there, and I'd like to see her."

"We'll go then." Hold the phone. I looked at him in confusion.

"We?"

"Yeah, I'm taking you to the Gala. You probably have a lot of shit you need to do for it, so why don't you do your thing for the rest of the day." I was still so hung up on the *we* part that I mumbled incoherently.

"As long as you are back in my bed tonight, do what you gotta do." He rapped his knuckles on the door twice then walked back down the stairs. Okay, even I had to admit to myself that Jake was pretty amazing. I laid back on the bed and listened to the sounds of all the animals outside. I could hear a roar from the big boy lion. I could hear a random howl from the wolves.

It was like being in *The Jungle Book*. I grabbed my bag and a few of my things, and went down to eat some lunch before I left. Binksie, who had been kind of scarce since our moment in the bedroom, was running around chasing a feathery ball. I watched him for a few minutes and laughed. Even though this cat was no tiny kitty, and neither were the big ones outside, they were a lot like the house cats normal people had in their homes. They moved like them, played like them. Some even purred. It was just amusing to me.

"Thank you. For not caring that I need to get ready for this thing tomorrow. And for going with me. I didn't really want to go alone." I did feel a little bad that Jake would be subjecting himself to that world. I looked him over now and was reminded how different our true worlds were. I was here, kind of on vacation, in a way. I would eventually go back home, and he would be here, doing this, every day.

"You don't have to though, if you don't want to. It's a real dressy thing, and the people aren't always so chill." I was back-pedaling and I knew it. Trying to keep my distance from the edge. Our worlds just didn't mesh.

"Cammy."I watched as he put yummy-looking turkey sandwiches on the table.

"Yeah?"

"Shut up."

"But!" I kept trying.

"Nope, eat your sandwich, then go do your Cammy thing. Just be back in my bed tonight." I felt like I just got schooled.

"Ok, well, if you get all miserable at the Gala, don't blame me. I tried," I grumbled as I sat down to eat.

"Thank you for feeding me." He was taking care of my every need. At least he was telling the truth in that little *I'm your alpha* speech. Jake was a man of his word. He gave Binksie some cut up turkey in a bowl, and then sat down to eat his sandwich. As I ate, I watched him, and thought of all things Jake.

I should add a word to Urban Dictionary.

Jake: The sexiest piece of man candy you will ever lay your eyes on. Purely undeniable, wicked with his tongue, the perfect mixture of dirty talk and sweetness that will curl your toes. Too bad I'm selfish and keeping him to myself. #DreamOnBitches.

Yep, that was his definition. I feel like if someone was watching my story on the big screen they would be saying, "What the hell is wrong with you, woman? Why are you fighting this? Jump on his dick and put a ring on it!" Hell, that was what I was saying to Rayne when she was fighting Arson's affections. But when it's your life, things are different. Not that the people of Sarasota, Florida were wolves, but in every elite society you had some predators.

On the other hand, Jake was a predator all on his own. And if anyone pissed him off, he could invite them over for dinner and throw them to the real wolves.

Maybe this would be all right. Jake was a big, handsome boy. I needed to stop worrying about this thing between us and simply enjoy it in the moment.

"So when are you getting Casey?" I wasn't going to fight him anymore on the Gala.

"I'll bring her over tonight." His eyebrow raised in question.

"I want to help with her. I mean, I know nothing about raising a baby tiger, but I can try." I wanted to mother the shit out of that little cub. My ovaries were marching around, holding parades, totally exploding with love for little Casey.

"You want to help take care of her?" he asked like he was trying to figure out what I said. It wasn't a puzzle.

"Yeah, I do. Something about her pulls at something in me. I understand if I'm not allowed to. Liability and all. Hell, shouldn't I have signed something about how my family shouldn't sue you in case I die, anyways?" And I was back to rambling.

"Probably." He winked, then nodded.

"You can help me. I'll show you what to do, just use your head. She can hurt you, even now," he stated. I wanted to jump up and down and do a little dance. I was going to help Casey grow up and be strong.

"Awesomesauce." I raised my cup of sweet tea to Jake, he lifted his and we clinked them together. We were classy like that.

After lunch, Jake went back out to do his stuff, and I hopped into Bambi, then drove to Rayne's apartment.

Chapter Seventeen

"Let me in, you hooker!" I knocked politely. Even though I had a key and used it frequently, I did not want to interrupt her and Arson having preggers sex.

"Good afternoon, Cammy." Arson opened the door with no shirt on.

Lord Jesus, there's a fire. I think I definitely got knocked up being around these hot men today.

"Go put a shirt on, Arson, you're distracting me from kidnapping your woman." I gave him a kiss on the cheek and walked in to see my bestie doing pregnant yoga in her living room.

"How's it going, my blossoming mother to be?" She looked really good. Healthy, glowing, and still in shape.

"Good." She breathed through her stretch. She had one leg behind her, while her body faced me and her other leg was bent underneath her. I would probably get stuck in a position like that.

"Awesome. I'm stealing you away from your lover to get pedicures for tomorrow." I sat down on her couch, making myself comfy. She smiled and got out of her position quickly.

"Sounds good, actually. I could use a good foot rubbing." She sat with her legs crossed.

"I rub your feet," Arson piped up from the kitchen.

"You're a lifesaver! But I still want someone to paint my toes, too." Then she whispered to me, "He sucks."

"Jake painted my toes pretty damn well," I commented, realizing my mistake after it was too late.

"So, things have progressed then?" Rayne looked really excited. She crawled over to me with her little belly swinging beneath her and sat beside me.

"I've decided to let things be for now. He's going with me to the Gala tomorrow."

"Oh, I get to meet Jake, the horse fister!" she exclaimed. I laughed at the nickname. Not sure he would ever live that down in my eyes. Arson simply shook his head as he walked into their bedroom.

"Yep, you get ready to get pampered. My girls are ready for us." I loved spending days like this with my Rayne. She was my person.

"Yes! Let me go put on a bra." She jumped up as quickly as her preggo body could manage and walked into the bedroom. She had a little waddle to her step, which made her look super cute. I couldn't wait to be a waddling preggo woman. She came out a moment later with kissed swollen lips and a happy look on her face. I said my goodbyes to Arson and we headed down to Bambi.

My girls took good care of us. Manicures, pedicures, and Rayne got a prenatal massage. I had to check over some stuff in the office so it was nice that she wasn't just sitting there waiting on me. Her sigh of contentment made me look up to see her walking into my office an hour later.

"I feel fantastic!" She plopped down on the little chair in front of my desk.

"Awesome. Did Cammy Jr. enjoy her massage? I hear they move a lot during those sessions."

"Yep, like a circus in there." She rubbed her baby belly. Envy coated my skin and I hated that feeling. I was happy for her.

"I want a baby." I spoke so soft it was a wonder she even heard me. I felt like I needed to get it off my chest. Rayne looked at me with a face that said *what the hell? Who are you?*

"I want a family, to be exact. It just hit me over the weekend and it's consuming my thoughts. I was just feeling envious of my best friend and it was the worst feeling I've ever had. I'm so sorry." I felt like ass now for even feeling that way.

"My best friend wants a family?" she repeated my statement. Did she not hear the part of where I was envious of her? I simply nodded

"Get the fuck on top of that, Cammy!" My face turned down. Uh, what?

"You need to get pregnant, like right now. And have the opposite of what I'm having, so they can be best friends growing up but then develop crushes on each other and get married! We could be family for real!" She literally started crying. The hormones must be going nuts inside her. My Rayne wasn't a crier.

"Well, easier said than done."

"I'm still betting on Jake. Let's hope he wins you over soon. You can be pregnant and miserable with me." I raised an eyebrow at that.

"Keep on betting, it's not a permanent thing between us, and you're not miserable, so shush. You're built for baby making." She rolled her eyes, but kept on smiling.
"Okay, I think it's time to go. I'm done here." I stood up and held out my hand to help her up. She grunted and played it up that she couldn't get out of the chair by herself, when we both knew she was very capable.

"Only ten more weeks to go!" she exclaimed.

"Yep, and you are still tiny as hell." She laughed and started her half-waddle, half-normal walk towards the door. Everyone blew us kisses as we left.

I dropped Rayne off at her apartment around 6:30 p.m. with promises of us getting ready tomorrow together. I drove the thirty minutes back to the rescue, and it looked like some hell had broken loose. I jumped out of my Beetle and walked over to Derek.

"What happened?" I asked with authority, as if I had a right to know what happened. What was wrong with me?

"Juno, the small lion, and her cage mate, Apollo, were playing a little rough; she needed some stitches. Things like this happen occasionally. She'll be ok. We will just have to keep an eye on them a little more in the future." He smiled at me and I felt a little more at ease.

"Oh. Hope she heals quickly then." Poor thing.

"I'm going to head inside. If you guys need help or whatever, let me know." I wanted to be useful, but then I looked down at my pretty, pink-colored nails and decided that maybe I should just hang out the rest of the night.

Didn't want to ruin anything. I let out a deep breath. I was losing my mind.

I walked into the house and noticed Binksie was creeping low to look around the couch in the living room. Odd. I stood there and watched as a little orange and black fuzzball came running around the corner of the couch, making Binksie take off with Casey chasing after him. It made me giggle, which made Jake walk down the stairs and sweep me into his arms. I wasn't really ready for his attack or the hell of a kiss he landed on my lips, but I welcomed it. I could definitely come home to this every day.

My body froze at that thought. Something in me was changing. Jake pulled back when I stopped kissing him and looked me over.

"Did you make dinner?" I choked out. He was eyeing me, trying to figure out what was going on in my head.

"I was just about to," he mumbled and I jumped out of his arms, faking excitement.

"Oh, good! I'll make us something. You've been cooking

this whole time; I need to make it up to you." I fake-smiled and walked into the kitchen. He let me have my space, so I turned on my cell phone for music and got to work on an awesome meal. Anything to distract me from realizing something big. Something I was in no way ready to admit.

Chapter Eighteen

I was swaying my hips and mixing the kick-ass chili I made when a song I had forgotten all about came through my little speaker. The strumming of the guitar was like having an epiphany. I grabbed the spoon I was stirring with, seductively licked it clean, and started singing the words into the spoon like it was a microphone.

I started belting out the lyrics to *Stacy's Mom* by Fountains of Wayne in the kitchen, and made a decision that, whenever I had a girl, because I would have one of course, that I would name her Stacy. I was going to be Stacy's mom. I would be a MILF. This song was going to be dedicated to me one day. It was now a life goal.

I swished my hair around like the rock star I was and started giving this song my everything. This was my song, after all. The song was coming to an end, I was mid-hair twirl and boob grab when I saw him leaning against the wall, watching me. BUSTED.

"Wonderful performance." He was fighting back laughter, with a big grin plastered on his face.

"Well, it's my song, sooo..." I finished my hair flip and gave my boob one last grab for his viewing pleasure.

"Your song?" His head turned to the side like a confused dog. It was cute.

"I'm going to be Stacy's mom. When I have a girl, I'm going to name her Stacy, and I will be her hot mom that her friends will want to see. A MILF." I gestured to my body like it was obvious they would want to see this hot mess. He shook his head but that laugh he was holding onto came out. It was going to come true one day; he could laugh all he wanted.

"Mad woman." He walked over to me and kissed me. It was a possessive type of kiss, a sweet kiss. One that said *I can't believe I like your brand of crazy, but I do. I really do.*

I kissed him, then smacked his ass with my spoon. He pulled back to look at me. *Did you really just smack me on the ass with a spoon?* was written all over his face. I had a *yeah, bitch, what are you going to do about it?* expression on my face.

We were having a conversation with our facial expressions and it was fun.

"The spoon did it all on its own. I had no control over it." I did it again and held a semi-serious face. I was in a playful mood and currently that meant smacking Jake on his delectable derriere. How he reacted would show me a lot about this thing between us, and by the look on his face, he was going to retaliate and I should run. Now.

I did.

I took off and headed up the stairs. He caught me at the last step, took me to the ground with my ass up in the air. I laughed loudly when he popped my ass with some sort of kitchen utensil. Spatula, maybe?

"Ah!" I cried out and laughed at the same time.

Then he abandoned his weapon and moved on to a far more painful form of torture: tickling me.

I thrashed and tried to get him back, or get away, but I was completely at his mercy. I saw the two cats were coming in to join the fun. Both Binksie and Casey were intrigued by my screams. They batted their paws at both Jake and me, not sure whose team they were on here.

I managed to turn my body around so he was facing me, wedged between my legs. He was still tickling me but I managed to get a jab of my finger in a few times, until he grabbed my wrists with one hand and pinned them above my head. Our faces were inches away from each other, and suddenly the playfulness left the air. Only thing left was the static sexual tension and emotions.

This would be a moment of declarations. I looked into his eyes and saw it in him, too. If he could say what he was thinking and not scare me off, he would.

"I know," I whispered to him. He didn't need to say it. From the look in his eyes, I understood it perfectly. I was *it* for him. I crawled out from under him and went back downstairs to turn the stove off. There was so much tension between us, and most of it was my doing. I was fighting this tooth and nail. I was off my rocker completely. Giving it a shot one minute, then running away the next.

Maybe I should have him just take me out back and put me out of my misery.

"Dinner's done," I announced and Jake came down the stairs, not acknowledging the big elephant in the kitchen. Or so I thought.

His arms wrapped around me, turning me in his embrace.
"What's going on in your head? Be straight with me, sweetheart. Remember?" I did say I was a straight shooter, and he wanted that from me, like I wanted it from him. He had been nothing but straight with me this whole time.

"This whole place scares me," I admitted. It was hard to say out loud, but I did it. His eyebrows pinched in the middle, he was confused.

"It's not the creatures. I'm not afraid I'm going to get bitten or anything."

"Elaborate, sweetheart." The dramatic flair in me reared her head. I pulled out of his arms and started my flailing.

"I could like it here and that scares me. This isn't me. This life isn't me. You're too damn amazing for your own good and your evil plan to keep me is working and it freaks me the hell out." There. I voiced my thoughts. Jake was digging his way inside me and I feared it would soon be too late to get him out.

"Maybe what you wanted isn't what you need. Maybe what you need is here. Change is okay, sweetheart. Change can reveal a future you never thought possible. Whatever you want, you can have." He took a step closer.

"I can give you the world, sweetheart." He meant it, but alas, that was where my problem lay. I didn't know what I wanted. I wanted him. But I wanted my salon, I wanted a family, I wanted to be a soccer mom. I didn't want to go back to my empty apartment when this week was over. But I wasn't sure I could stay here, either.

"I don't know what I want." I gave it to him straight.

"I know I want to eat this chili, though. I worked hard on it. So let's just eat, and go from there. One step at a time." I grabbed a bowl and loaded it with some corn chips, cheese, sour cream, and chili, then handed it to him.

He grabbed the bowl and sat at the table. I made my own, then joined him. He complimented my cooking and we chatted about what we would do tomorrow for the Gala, which started at 6 p.m. I promised to help him with a few things in the morning, but then I was going to head over to Rayne's to get ready. I told Jake I would meet him at the Mote Marine Aquarium, then ride back with him after it was over.

"I know a good place you can get a tux, if you need one." I doubted Jake had a tux lying around. If it wasn't a Henley shirt, boots, or jeans, he probably didn't ever wear it.

"I've got it covered." He winked and got a beep from Derek that they needed him over by Koda's enclosure. He looked at me like he wanted to stay and felt bad for leaving, but honestly, it was ok. I could play with the kitties, read, or pass out. I was sort of tired.

"Go, I'll be here." I stretched my arms over my head, and yawned. Maybe I was more tired than I thought.

"Be good. Don't let Casey destroy the house too much." He stood and put his bowl in the sink before heading out. I sat there and watched Binksie and Casey lying on one of the dog beds together. Two peas in a pod. I finished eating my chili, then went upstairs to shower and dress in my jammies, a simple shirt and shorts again. I spent the next couple hours watching the cats play together— it was wildly entertaining.

Jake came back in and put Casey in a large crate he had set up in the living room in the corner. It was her bedtime. She went peacefully into her quarters and I laid on the couch with Binksie and told them funny stories about my life.

Jake had once again carried me up to the bed some point in the night, because I woke up snuggled in his arms. Keeping my eyes closed, I simply listened to his even breaths, and felt his chest move with every inhale. It was peaceful enough that I fell back asleep.

When I finally woke back up again, the sun was shining brightly through the windows. Jake was missing from the bed, but Binksie had taken his spot.

"Where'd he go?" I asked the giant kitty. Binksie continued to snooze and didn't even bother to acknowledge menthe clock on his side of the bed glowed 9

162

a.m. He let me sleep in? I told him I would help with stuff. On the other hand, I felt very refreshed and rested. Maybe I needed it.

Chapter Nineteen

"Morning." The man of the hour came walking in with coffee. I squealed in delight. Yeah, I squealed.

"Thank you!" I gripped the handle of the cup and smelled the delicious aroma. Heavenly.

"Thought you'd like to sleep in. I have to make a video today and thought you'd want to watch. After that, you can go get ready with your friend." He looked fine on the outside but I could feel something stewing underneath.

"You okay?" I took a sip of my coffee. I moaned, it was so good.

"Yeah." He rubbed the back of his neck nervously.

"Uh huh," I mumbled into the cup. Something was up, but he wasn't ready to talk about it. That's fine. I had plenty of those moments lately. I trusted that soon he would tell me whatever was bothering him.

"Finish your cup, get dressed, then meet me outside." He rubbed Binksie's ears, then walked briskly out of the room. I did as he said and was ready in my cute jeans, boots, and a pretty, blue short-sleeved shirt. He had the ATV ready and I hopped on, arms around his waist.

We drove over to the bobcat area first, where a couple of interns were setting things up with a camera.

"Are you doing a show?"

"We do videos of everything that happens on the rescue and put them on YouTube. It helps educate the public, and keeps up interest in what we do. Today is box day." He pulled up and stopped.

Autumn and Helen were there, waiting with thumbs up at Jake. They rolled their eyes when they saw me get off the ATV with him, but otherwise kept to themselves. Jake walked over to the enclosure and stood in front of it. I noticed two other rescue workers on the other side of the cage with their thumbs up.

"Okay, ready?" Autumn asked Jake and the person holding the camera. They all signaled that they were okay and I saw the little red light on the camera blink on.

"You know how house cats love boxes? Well, it turns out so do the big ones!" Jake beamed at the camera and then a bobcat was let loose from its eating nook, heading straight for the box. The camera person moved so they could get a good angle of the cat sniffing and scratching at the box. I laughed a little when the bobcat tried to crawl into the box just like I'd seen normal kitties do.

We went around to each of the cat enclosures, and watched as each of them investigated and played with their own box. It was really fun to watch, and cool that everyone who looked online could watch and have fun, too. When the fun was over, I kissed Jake goodbye and left to get all of my things from my house so I could go get ready with Rayne.

"Okay, all set." I finished the last bit of blush on Rayne's cheeks and took a step back. My little blossom was utterly beautiful and ready to wiggle into her cute purple dress. I did my makeup and hair while she took a nap; the only thing left for me was the dress and accessories, as well.

"Okay, no looking!" When I dolled her up, I never let her look in the mirror until she was a completely finished product. That way she saw herself in all her glamour, not piece by piece. I unzipped her garment bag and helped her get into the Grecian-style dress that flowed over her belly and wrapped over her left shoulder. My eyes started to glisten seeing her all pregnant and looking like a goddess. I hopped into my dress quickly, then went back to her.

"Rayne, babe, you are gorgeous." I helped her get to the full-length mirror in her room and took a step back.

"Wow. Arson is not going to let me leave the house!" she giggled.

I would probably have to drag them both out the door. Moving in next to her, I looked over my own princess outfit. I was wearing a black floor length dress, but instead of the Grecian look, I went with something different. My shoulders and neck were exposed, thanks to the open neckline that wrapped around my quarter-length sleeves.

The material was glittery, but soft. A four-inch ribbon started at the back seam from the zipper and came to a square bow in the front of my waist. The soft material flowed down from there. All I needed were some earrings to compliment my smoky black eye shadow and red lipstick. My red hair was pulled back into a low bun with little wisps around my face.

Rayne's pretty green eyes stood out, thanks to the golden eye shadow that coated them. But it wasn't her eye shadow that was standing out now—it was the look on her face.

"What?" What was her deal?

"You are so getting pregnant tonight. That wild man of yours is going to put a baby in you." She laughed at me when I rolled my eyes.

"Those pregnancy hormones are affecting your brain. No babies will be planted tonight. I am on the pill, thank you very much. Not until it's planned." I put in some earrings and handed Rayne a pair as well.

"Uh huh." I ignored her comment and as expected, wound up having to drag both of them out of the apartment by their toes.

"So I was telling Larry the other day that it was silly to buy a Porsche. So we bought a Range Rover instead. Very responsible of us. Now we will have room to fit the boy in the backseat." The wife of a plastic surgeon was talking to me, rattling on about their new son, who the nanny took care of, and how they bought a Range Rover over a Porsche. I plastered a smile on my face.

"Excuse me one moment, I need to go to the restroom." I walked away and headed off in a different direction. I glanced over at Arson and Rayne, they were working the room just like I was. We could be ourselves to a certain extent, but I was no millionaire. If someone happened to get pissy and complain to the right person, causing the closing of my salon for some reason, I would be screwed. All of my girls would be out of a job. I would be okay for a while, but I would have to get a job somewhere. Arson and Rayne were the same. They had money, but other people depended on them to play nice.

Wanting somewhere quiet I stepped into the little alcove to the shark tank. Fish swam by peacefully while being surrounded by a couple of sharks. Story of my life.

"Hanging with the good sharks. Smart, sweetheart." I didn't turn at his voice. I'd been at the Gala for an hour and a half and he hadn't shown up. I was beginning to think he wasn't going to come.

"These ones looked safer." In truth, I bet people go in those tanks all the time. Cleaning it, moving things around. The sharks probably just went on with their shark lives. The rest of the sharks in this aquarium were on the lookout for blood in the water.

"I've been waiting all day to see you dressed up. Now turn around, beautiful." His voice was calm but demanding. I took in a short, but deep breath and did as he said. He was standing five feet behind me, looking drop-dead gorgeous in a black tux. Both of our gazes roamed over our appearance. Jake in a tux was beautiful, but oddly, I felt myself longing for the animal Jake.

"I like your other look better." You could tell he was toned underneath the suit, but his normal attire made him look all muscled, warm-blooded man. Tuxed Jake looked like a high- powered someone from the city. He still had an air of authority, even if he was uncomfortable. It was the alpha in him that he talked so much about.

"Good to know, only words I have for how you look tonight is, I'm glad you're mine. Shall we?" He held his hand out to me and I accepted it.

"I thought you were going to chicken out." We walked back out towards the crowds of people.

"Had a branch fall on one of the enclosure fences. I had to fix it up before I could head over." Well, that shut me up. The rescue was his life; it came first. It had to.

"Well, thank you for coming," I told him as a man and his wife, whose names escaped me, walked up to us.

"Jake Wild! I'll be damned, never thought I'd see you at something like this in a million years." The gentleman had brown hair and wrinkles around his blue eyes. He was fairly in shape, and dressed in an Armani suit. His female guest was several years younger, wearing a short blue cocktail dress and eyeing up Jake with her overkill make-uped eyes.

"James, pleasure to see you again. Have you met my date, Cammy Jennings? She owns Prism Salon on St. Armand's." Jake's posture was strong, but I was confused how they knew each other.

"Oh, I've been dying to go to that salon. It looks so swanky." The date squealed. That was nice of her to say, but swanky...? Not sure about that.

"No, I have not. Ms. Jennings, pleasure." He held out his hand, which I shook in return. Our introductions died and there was an awkward silence spreading.

"Sorry, I'm just so surprised to see you. Marlene is going to blow when she sees America's most eligible bachelor is here. Better dig your claws in deep with him, because I think we have company." James was having a spout of the nervous giggles. It was awkward and weird, to say the least.

Chapter Twenty

"Jake Wild. Ever since you left the city and moved down to our little town, I have been waiting to see what you have been up to." A supermodel-looking woman wearing a red dress, with curled blonde hair and who was probably close to my age, walked right up to Jake and kissed him on the cheek. She did not care that I was holding his hand or that she pushed the other couple out of the way.

"Marlene," Jake acknowledged her but kept his face void of any emotions. I did not like that.

"I'm Cammy. Nice to meet you," I said, interrupting her roving eyes.

"Oh, pardon, didn't see you there. I'm Marlene Debarue, James's sister. We own all of the Rue Diamonds in the country." She bitch-smiled at me. Like I cared. I was more of a sapphire girl, anyway. James was rolling his eyes like she was the bratty little sister.

"Wonderful to meet you." It was hard for me to reel in the bitchiness, but I was succeeding thus far.

"I'm so excited you have resurfaced. It's been, what, five years? What have you been up to? We must get together, for old times' sake." Oh dear God, did Jake penetrate this skanky woman's vagina? Ew.

"I've been running a rescue for exotic animals," he commented, but didn't elaborate.

"Animals?" She gasped at the word.

"Yes. All sorts." He was short in his answer. I could tell he wasn't too happy to be around this woman, either. James and his date were watching their conversation with absolute attention.

"I can't picture you around animals. I mean, you're Jake Wild." She was looking at him like she was trying to figure him out. If I was being honest, this conversation was starting to confuse me, and I didn't like that.

"So how do you two know each other?" I asked, voicing the question I had been asking internally since she walked up.

"We played in the same circles back in the day. Much has changed but it seems you still fill out a tux very well." She turned back to him and eyed him up. Ew. I was done with her eye-fucking him.

"That he does. You should see him at the rescue, talk about melting panties!" I fanned myself and Jake covered his laugh with a cough. Marlene's eyes darted to mine.

"Cammy, may I have a word with you?" She wrapped her hand around mine and pulled me away from Jake. Not wanting to make a huge scene, I allowed.

"Are you and Jake an item? I must know." She stopped and turned to me, a few feet away from our little circle.

"Yes, he's mine." Declaration made, bitch.

"Well, as you probably know, Rue Diamonds is worth millions. Name your price to leave Jake, and I will handle it." My jaw dropped. Her face said she was completely serious, but surely she was joking.

"Uh, no." It was all I could utter, in my shock.

"Honestly, Cammy, you have no idea who you are even with. Jake Wild needs a woman of sophistication. A woman who can handle his personality, his home life. I understand what all he goes through, being of his stature. You, my dear, have no clue." She stood up higher, like she was proving her point of superiority. Fuck that.

"Honestly, Marlene," I used the sweet tone she just used with me, "you can go fuck yourself. Jake is mine, and trust me, I handle him just fine."

She leaned in closer. It was an aggressive stance.

"I could ruin you, you know. I get what I want and I want Jake. He's been gone from my life too long, and now I want him. I will do whatever it takes to get him."

Did this bitch just threaten me?

"Hell, no, you did not just threaten me, bitch. I may not be as bad ass as Rayne, but I can sure as hell choke a bitch up in here." I was starting to turn on the flail when strong arms wrapped around me.

"I'm sorry, Jake, she just started getting attitude with me. I tried to calm her down, but she just threatened me." Her little pouty pink lips poked out. OH. HELL. NO! I tried to reach her with my hands, but Jake pulled me back. "Marlene. I suggest you leave." His voice was harsh, but I didn't flinch hearing it.

"Me? She's the one that threatened to attack me," she whined.

"She just tried to *buy you from me*. Then threatened to ruin me. Which, by the way, try it. See what happens." That was a bluff. She could probably bring my business down.

"I did not—" Marlene tried to get in another word, but Jake cut her off.

"Leave. If you try to touch Cammy's life in any way, I WILL ruin you. You know I can. Cammy is my future and you'll damn well treat her like fucking royalty. I mean it, Marlene. I will destroy your pampered life." His voice left no trace of confusion in it. He meant it. But how the hell could he ruin her? Set his bear on her? I was down with that, but the look on her face said it all—she was scared that he would do exactly what he said he would.

"Come on, Marlene." James came and collected his sister.

"Sorry about her, Jake. She will stay away." They walked away and I noticed Rayne and Arson walking over towards us.

"Cammy! Are you okay? We heard some shouting." Rayne looked full of concern and Arson was giving Jake the eye. But more like in a way that men talked to each other telepathically: Like, *everything ok?* face. *Yeah, I solved it* face.

"Yeah, some bitch just tried to pay me off so she could date Jake. Insane in the membrane for sure." I shook my head. I was done with this party. My mood was officially killed.

"Can we go? I don't want to be here anymore." I looked up to Jake with pleading eyes. His face was hard. I wanted to soothe him and bring back the fun Jake that tickled me on the stairs.

"Oh, can we go dancing? I haven't gotten to wear a pretty dress in a while. It would be nice to get some fun out of it." Rayne rubbed her baby belly a little and I thought it sounded like a great idea.

"Sounds fabulous to me. Boys?" I looked at both of the sexier-than-sin men in our lives.

"Fine." Both men agreed.

I hopped into the car with Rayne and Arson, and Jake drove behind us to a dancing hot spot.

Rayne and I danced like fools in our fancy dresses and we couldn't give any shits about it.

I did the sprinkler and the running man, and Rayne discoed. We were having a blast while Arson and Jake sat off to the side and watched us, chatting with each other. No other man came near us because of the bubble of *stay the fuck away* both of our men had created around us. Marlene and her stupid threat were long forgotten after I had a pretty blue drink and started dancing. But as much as I loved dancing with Rayne, I wanted to get Jake on the floor. Rayne must have been feeling the same way, because she gave me a nod in their direction and I grinned in agreement. We both stalked over to them, and dragged them out to dance with us just in time for a fun song to come through the speakers.

It was upbeat and dirty. The song was about Marvin Gaye's *Let's Get It On*. But hell if it wasn't fun to sway to. I laced my fingers through Jake's and started moving our hands together, trying to get him to loosen up. His smirk grew and he started swaying a little bit. I laughed and turned, wrapping our joined hands around my chest. Wiggling my ass against him, and swaying with our hands held against me. Finally, he started to give me what I wanted. We smiled and moved in sync, enjoying the moment.

Dancing and goofing off in this moment made me realize I was giving up my fight. I wanted to have fun in life. You never knew when things could end for you, so you might as well have that dance with a sexy man, and give life your all. I unwound our hands and turned so I was facing him, my arms wrapped around his neck. He was perfection and I was a dumbass if I didn't see where we could go, plain and simple.

"Take me home, Jake." My resolve was set and Jake could tell right away.

"Home." He confirmed and pulled me in for a kiss. This was home. His lips, his arms, wherever he was, I would be home.

I pulled back, eager to get a move on, and set out to tell Rayne we were leaving. When I saw them dancing, my heart swelled. Arson hand his hands on her stomach; it was like they were dancing as a family of three already. I hated to disrupt their moment together. Thankfully, Rayne's eyes found mine and I gestured with my thumb towards the door that we were leaving. She gave me two thumbs up and pointed at her belly then me and I just turned toward the door. There would be no sperm and eggs hooking up tonight. Now vagina and cock, those two were going to be getting down to business for a few hours, hopefully.

Chapter Twenty-one

Jake led the way to his truck, which turned out to not be his normal truck but something way different.

"Whose car is this?" I asked, in a stupor. I was confused. He had opened the door of a car that was a freaking beast.

"What? Don't approve of my Eleanor?" He smirked and held out his hand to help me get in the car. Once we were both in the car, I rubbed my hands over the fine leather, and inside details. This was one hot car.

"Eleanor?" That sounded so familiar.

"Yeah, this beauty is a 1967 Shelby GT 500, a beast of a woman. The movie *Gone In Sixty Seconds* named this car Eleanor. It stuck in my head, and I always knew I wanted one." He turned on the sexy, candy apple red muscle car and we took off.

Was it possible to be turned on by a car? Because I was purring along with her.

"I want to have sex in this car... on it, all over it. Is that wrong?" I asked Jake, with a serious face. I heard him groan and grip the steering wheel.

"I know it's probably a really expensive car, but it just makes me really hot," I continued, running my fingers along the leather.

"Sweetheart." I looked at his face that spoke volumes. He was seconds away from pulling this car over and fogging up the windows. He was warning me. Maybe he knew this about me by now, or not, but I wasn't much at heeding warnings. I rubbed the leather seductively, arching my back and putting on a show in the passenger seat.

Feeling like torturing him a little, I unbuckled myself and moved toward him. My tongue flicked his ear before sucking it into my mouth, giving it a little nip. I felt his arms harden beneath my breasts. I moved my mouth over his trimmed jaw, and onto his neck. I felt the terrain below us change from smooth pavement to a dirt road. I smiled and continued my assault on the driver of this beast. My hands went to his chest, running along the seam of the tux.

The car was speeding down the dirt road. I felt like a couple of teenagers on the run for a place to get dirty. God, I hoped that was true. Suddenly I was flung across the car by him turning the wheel hard and fishtailing to a stop. Hitting the side of the car hurt a little, but when Jake turned and lunged for me, that little tinge of pain turned to molten pleasure. His mouth attacked mine with the desire of a starving man.

"Get out of the car," he growled at me. I whimpered at his command with anticipation. With a smug smile on my lips, I pulled on the handle behind me and crawled out of the car. I watched as he crawled his big body out the passenger side and stood before me.
He gripped behind my neck and pulled my lips to his. Our tongues danced and my hands roamed. Then his lips left mine and he bent down to get a grip on the bottom of my dress, slowly his hands moved up my legs with the dress in tow.

A shiver broke out over my skin with his soft touch. When his hands reached the bottom of my ass, he gripped and lifted me up and onto his body. Instinctively, my legs wrapped around him. I was beyond hot for this man, so I started ripping his shirt open and kissing every part of him I could touch. He lit me on fire and I was going to burn us both from the heat. He set me down in front of the car and spun me around, his fingers quickly finding the zipper to my dress and pulling it down enough to expose my breasts to the summer air. I looked around for the first time, a little nervous as to where we were.

We were covered by darkness but by that storage shed where Jake's mouth made love to my pussy on the ATV. It must have been where he kept this car.

"I want your tits imprinted into the hood of my car, sweetheart." He nudged me down and my face was plastered to the car, ass in the air. It was hot from being driven hard by a horny man, but it wasn't burning me in any way. He lifted the skirt of my dress, a soft breeze caressing my ass cheeks, telling me that I was out there for his viewing.

A yelp flew from my lips when I felt his teeth bite down on my butt cheek, his hand palming the other. My breathing started turning ragged. He was something completely different than I had ever experienced, and I was beyond ready for the animal in him to be set free.

When his fingers traced the seam of my panties and his tongue followed, I was moaning so loud, not giving one fuck who heard me.

"Jake," I pleaded.

"I know what you need, sweetheart. Remember? Fast." Pushing aside my panties, his finger plunged into me and started moving so fast I was seeing beautiful stars, already so close.

"Slow." He slowed his pace and I wanted to cry.

"Hard." He bit my clit and I cried out for the mixture of pleasure and pain. This man was driving me wild.

"Soft." His tongue caressed me, and I was ready to beg with everything I had. I would give him anything he wanted, as long as he gave me what I needed.

His fingers and tongue retreated. I heard the sound of his zipper going down and felt such relief that I was sure my body sagged into the metal beneath me. My panties were slid down my legs, and the sound of a condom packet ripping echoed around us. Or at least in my head it did. My hands felt around, tried to grip the raised edge in the middle of the hood for support. I felt the head of him by my entrance and my hips moved towards him, needing him like nothing else.

"Who does this belong to?" he growled, gripping my hair and pulling me back as he leaned over so our cheeks met. I cried out, but only from the animalistic dominance he was giving me.

He pressed the crown of himself inside me, then pulled out.

"Who do you belong to?" he growled again. He wanted to claim me as much as I wanted him to.

"You, Jake! You own me." No sooner had the words left my mouth than he was driving himself inside me, punishing my pussy with unimaginable euphoria. Over and over he pushed me further onto the car, his cock hitting my G-spot with a precision that was going to have me screaming his name in seconds.

"You're mine, sweetheart. Never a doubt that you'd be mine. So perfect," he whispered against my ear before I went back to being smushed on the hood. His hands gripped my hips as he drove me into oblivion. I screamed out in release, my whole body shattered, and my mind went blank.

My legs quivered, and I scratched at the hood. He kept going until suddenly his teeth latched onto that tender spot where my shoulder and neck met, and growled as he came, spurring me into another spiral of orgasmic bliss.

It was undoubtedly the most erotic moment in my life. Jake was everything I thought he would be, and more. So much more.

"You're going to have to carry me. I think I've lost feeling in my legs from your dick crushing my spine from my vagina," I breathed dramatically. I heard him chuckle behind me and gently pull out. I stayed molded to the car while he pulled my panties back up into place, zipped me back up, and scooped me into his arms. I snuggled in against his ripped-open shirt.

"I think I could go into an orgasm coma right now," I murmured against him. I was completely jellified, and utterly happy. He set me on top of an ATV that was parked next to the big shed.

"Still with me here?" he asked. I knew he meant something other than physically here with him. He wanted to make sure I hadn't change my mind, that I was still here with him together, that he was mine and I was his.

"I'm yours, Jake," I told him in earnest. I don't know how it was going to work, but I was going to try my hardest to make it happen. I wanted to be with him, therefore I would be.   He held in whatever emotions he was feeling at my statement, then turned back to the car and parked it inside the building. After he closed the door, I bunched up the skirt of my dress and held it in front of me so it wouldn't get stuck in the wheels or anything. I scooted up and patted for Jake to sit behind me. He shook his head at first, but then hopped on behind me.

"Okay, show me how to work this thing?" I asked him, eagerness flowing through me.

"I thought you were in an orgasm coma. Not sure you are fit to drive." I didn't have a retort to that. My brain was foggy, but I knew I was capable of handling this mini-beast.

"Shush and teach me how to drive." I turned and kissed his lips really quickly. He told me what to do, step by step, and then we were on our way. Probably only going two miles an hour, or slower. I was kind of scared, but I ventured on. We passed by some of the nocturnal creatures and I will say their glossy eyes were kind of creepy as they watched us pass.

Chapter Twenty-two

As we inched closer to the lodge, I felt like a total badass. I turned the machine off and was surprised when Jake hopped off and scooped me up, carrying me up the stairs and into the house.

"What? Are we crossing the threshold here?" I laughed at the ridiculousness of him carrying me into the house, and then up the stairs.

"Gotta make sweet love to my woman now," he winked at me and I was smiling from ear to ear.

I expected him to take me into the bedroom for round two, but instead we were heading into the spare bedroom. My eyes zeroed in on the mirror and my whole body shook from the memory of his words about that mirror.

He set me down facing the full-length freestanding mirror and stood behind me. I looked a little like a hot mess. A hot mess that had been deliciously screwed on the hood of a sexy car. Softly his fingers unzipped me, then slowly, with both hands, he moved my sleeves down, baring my breasts, then my navel, before the whole dress pooled around my toes. His chest rumbled behind me, making me hyperaware of the intimacy of this moment. My eyes met with his as they committed my body into memory.

"I need to see you," I whispered to him. His eyes flew to mine before he slid off his tattered shirt and jacket. I felt so small standing in front of him. You could see his chest, arms, and sides silhouetting around me.

"So beautiful." His lips touched my neck, warm breath caressing my skin. My hands went to his head. Holding him there against me. There were no words that could be uttered to improve this moment. His hands ravished my breasts, teasing my pink tips, then flowing along the little curves of my waist. When his finger brushed against my clit, my nails dug into his thick brown hair. He teased me gently, making my hips move towards him, needing everything he had to give me.

Goosebumps rose over my skin when his other hand left to undo his slacks. We were completely open to each other, both baring our skin and souls. No boundaries. His mouth licked down my spine and back up. My hands joined his, lacing them together as he moved over my body as one. When he placed my hands against the sides of the mirror stand, I knew this moment was going to be life-changing. One strong finger ran down the line of my spine and slowly moved back up. I shook with need but stayed silent, my eyes trying to find the man silhouetted behind me. All the lights were off in the house, but I could see him by the moonlight coming in through the window.

I felt him prod my entrance and wiggled for him to take me again. It was all I wanted. He and I, like this. I felt my heart clench and my brain clicked. I'd known this man for not even a week, and he proved to be everything I didn't even know I wanted. He was the perfect match for me. No matter how hard I wanted to fight it, I was falling in love with him. Our eyes met and in that second I knew my thoughts were written on my face. He could see it. He growled and pushed into me, my toes lifting up to keep myself rooted on him, just as he said they would. My head dropped from feeling a shiver course through me, and my insides clenched.

"Eyes," he commanded, and I gave my gaze back to him. I expected him to go full force into me but I was wrong. Slowly he slid out to the tip then back in. The pace was so slow, it was like a sweet torture. With every thrust, I inched closer and closer toward the mirror. Gasps of my breath filled the room, mixed with a lion's roar outside the window. The soundtrack to my new life. He pulled completely out and turned me around, lips melding to mine with uninhibited need. He walked us backwards until the back of my knees hit the bed and I went down onto my back. Jake was there with me, sliding into me without haste.

That night Jake Wild made love to me. He was my everything. He'd seen it all, and he was giving me all he had. Sweat, groans, and tangled sheets were burned into my memory. We fell asleep wrapped in our embrace of acceptance. This was love; we were love.

When I woke in the morning, the sun was shining and there was a glass of water, a croissant, and a note on the nightstand. I couldn't feel my legs again, but this time I knew it was because there was a Binksie lying on them. I reached over to the note and read the cursive letters. Jake had lovely penmanship.

Had to take care of an emergency. Have breakfast, take a shower, and join me at the wolves. Time to meet the pack.

Always something happening at the rescue. It was never ending, in a wonderful way. Jake was helping creatures that needed him. He was acting as their voice, when they had no words. I took a sip of the water and grabbed the pastry. Lying back on the pillow, I ate my pastry and smiled like a goof about how my life was taking a sharp turn I had never expected. I guess I should thank my niece for this change. If it were not for her party and the damn wallaby, I wouldn't have run into Jake. Maybe a nice shopping trip with her auntie would be reward enough.

Soon I felt sated from the bread and more than a little excited to see Jake again. I blew Binksie a kiss before nudging him off my legs. He looked at me with those piercing serval eyes, but politely moved. Naked, I checked the windows to see that Jake had closed the sheer curtains, but still a little paranoid, I wrapped myself in the sheet and ran to the bathroom in Jake's room. Grabbing my phoneme saw I had notifications from a few people, but knew my salon wasn't open yet and I wanted to be in my little post-glorious-night ignorance. I turned on some music, since I did almost everything listening to music, and jumped into the shower. He had such a nice shower.

Chapter Twenty-three

I had just finished washing the conditioner out of my hair and started brushing my teeth when another tune I hadn't heard in a while started playing.

I looked at my phone like it was some sort of mind reader. First *Stacy's Mom* and now this. But as the voice of Akon started to mix in with the shower's steam I couldn't help but give into it.

I started mumbling the words to *I Just Had Sex* by Lonely Island as I finished cleaning my teeth. I spit out the paste just as the chorus started and I sang along with the ridiculous lyrics to this song about having just had sex. Which I did. Which made me put my Cammy flair into it because it was fitting.

My toothbrush was my mic. I gyrated, and rolled my hips. I sang to the people of the world that had just had sex, like me, making a mental note to sing this song at karaoke one night. I closed my eyes and did what I did best, giving the performance my best. I was just finishing the final high notes when I had a feeling I was being watched. My eyes opened, toothbrush mic still dangling above my tilted head, to Jake standing against the door jamb, watching me. AGAIN.

"Do you have cameras watching me so you won't miss any of my private performances?" I mean, seriously. He caught me every time!

"Just great timing," he chuckled. I washed my face and put my toothbrush in its new shower holder before exiting the shower, turning off my phone before another song could snare me in its grasp.

"Great timing, my ass. You're a secret agent, spying on innocent girls while they sing and dance. Creeper." I was teasing.

"Especially ones that sing about having sex, and that it felt so good." Cue embarrassment. Yep, I was totally singing like a fool, naked, about having sex. My cheeks grew warm, but I tried to pull off a kick-ass come back.

"Yeah, well, my fingers are pretty talented, so they deserved some praise." Nailed it. I pretended to drop the mic in front of his face. He was smiling at me, obviously not at all bothered by my posturing. He was like a proud little peacock, standing there. I grabbed my towel and dried off, changing the subject so I wouldn't dig another embarrassing hole for myself.

"I thought you were waiting by the wolves." I walked into the room and started getting dressed while Jake watched me.

"My watch alarm went off that the cameras caught you doing a dance, so I got here as quickly as possible." He was fighting back laughter and I wanted to die. Once I was fully clothed in a pair of cute tan shorts, my boots, and a blue T-shirt, I turned to him.

"Okay, let's go, smart ass." I walked out of the room and down the stairs. I knew he followed behind me but I was on a roll so I kept on walking, out of the house and towards the wolves' area.

"So what happened this morning?" I asked him as we came to a stop.

"Bobcat got shot in the leg by a punk with an arrow. The parents of the kid brought it to us. We have a rehabilitation area, so Doc fixed it up and put it in a temporary home for now. We'll release it in a week or so, whenever Doc says he's good to go." His arms circled around me from behind, and like a cat doused in water, I lost all of my fight.

"Oh, I'll have to make it a pretty toy or something." And the crazy thing was, I meant it. I wanted to bring a little joy into that poor kitty's life.

Over the next hour, Jake introduced me to the wolf pack. There were seven of them. The top dog, if you will, was bonded with Jake and listened to him. But there were some that kept their distance. Most of the animals at the rescue were completely hands off. For a select few, Jake or Derek could get in the habitat with them. One of the wolves growled at me, and I might have peed a little. Well, that was a lie, but it made me jump enough that I could have!

We left the wolves, and went to go check in on the new bobcat. She was doing well. Very skittish, but she hadn't really had any human contact, so I couldn't blame her there. We kept walking and checking on all the animals, making sure the workers didn't need anything from us, then went to go get my precious baby, Casey. Jake carried the wiggly kitty back to the lodge and I talked to her, telling her about how Jake and I finally got together, and I was going to see her as much as possible, even when she went into her big kitty habitat. Her big blue eyes watched me, and I swear I saw a wink, so I know she got me.

When we made it back to the lodge, Jake got everything set up for Casey, making sure nothing breakable was in her reach and covering all the furniture, because those claws of hers were starting to do some damage. I ran up the stairs to check those notifications on my phone, but got distracted watching Jake put a baby gate on the stairs. Cute.

I could see him doing that for his babies, so they wouldn't fall down the stairs. His kids. My kids? Having kids with Jake wouldn't be so bad. He would be a really good daddy. I smiled as I turned to go get my phone, feeling all sorts of jitters from thinking about Jake as a daddy.

"Holy hell!" I was shocked at how many notifications, calls, and emails I had missed. Were zombies attacking and I didn't know about it?

Rayne, my sister, my mother, the salon, Mary. Everyone had tried to reach me. Even though I should have read everyone else's stuff first, I read Rayne's message. What if something happened to the baby?

Rayne- Babe. You need to read this.

There was a link below her text. I clicked on it to see the headline

Sorry, Ladies, Jake Wild is finally taken.

Uh, say what? I kept reading.

Notorious millionaire, and bad boy gone animal rescuer has been scooped up by a saucy redhead.

As you know, women all over the country have been waiting in the wings ever since Jake gave up his New York bad boy image and traded it to help exotic animals in Southwest Florida.

Son to Bernard and Lenora Wild, Jake lived up to his name of being exactly that, WILD.As the oldest child of four, his net worth was over fifty million and counting. But then one day, he traded that life of luxury to help animals in need—which only made the female population swoon even harder.

Jake was seen at the local Aquarium Gala with the redhead, then was spotted dancing at the club Yimka with said woman as well, before they sped off in his Shelby GT 500.

Who is this mystery woman who has apparently tamed the Wild man himself?

I sat there staring at the article with wide eyes and confusion. There was a horrible picture of us together, dancing sweetly. Someone must have taken it on the sly. Jake Wild, bad boy, millionaire.

They had to be wrong. Jake was so down to earth, although he had to be a little on the nutty side to want to be around my bag of crazy. But, seriously, besides the GT, he drove a truck that looked okay, but not millionaire worthy.

Although, he did run this place, and it kind of made sense. I think he said the care and feeding of just one tiger alone was ten thousand a year. And the rescue sat on 200 acres. I'm sure he got donations, and other state assistance, but if he was loaded, then he would be able to take care of most of it himself.

All these little dots in my head started connecting. What happened at the Gala, the car, piece by piece, things I had overlooked were making sense. I glanced through the rest of my notifications to see they were all about Jake and me. Nobody had died. Yet.

Chapter Twenty-four

I tossed my phone on the bed and marched down to have a few words with the bad boy millionaire in question. The baby gate stopped me briefly, but once I figured that out, I was back to my search. I found him in the living room watching Casey and Binksie play.

"We need to talk." I walked up to him and straddled his lap so he couldn't go anywhere. When he put his hands on my hips, I remembered why this was a bad decision. He could turn our talk into something dirtier.

"Who are you, Jake?"

"Jake," he answered flatly.

"You know what I mean. I feel like I don't know the man I'm in love with, and it's freaking me out. My phone nearly exploded from all the notifications from people flipping out about me apparently being with a bad boy millionaire from New York. I mean, I feel like I'm on an episode of PUNKED or something." I didn't flail this time. I watched his face as he took in what I said.

"I'm sorry." He looked me straight on, no shame or regret in his eyes.

"So it's true. You're some big hot shot wild man from the city. You're a millionaire?" The last part I could have cared less about, it was just the fact that I didn't know.

"Does it matter?"

"The money? No." My answer was absolute and quick.

"I just want to know who you are." He pulled me in for a kiss then leaned his forehead against mine, eyes closed.

"This is me. Who I was before, is not who I am now. Right now I am just a man who wants to be with the woman he loves and have her love him in return."

My breathing stopped. I knew how he felt. I could feel it with every gaze, with every touch. But hearing it did something to me. Some wall I had unknowingly built just crumbled.

"You have my love," I whispered to him. We were moving so fast, everything was a blur around us. He had me completely, every breath, and every heartbeat.

"Will you tell me about your life? Old, new, and everything in between?" I asked as I laid my head against his shoulder. I wanted to know everything about this man that I could. We chatted for a few hours, learning everything we could. Favorite colors. Mine was orange, his was red. My favorite movie was *Pitch Perfect*, his was *300*.

He grew up in New York, where his dad was a big hot shot in advertising, his mother was a doctor, and his sisters were doing their own thing. After one sister had a big sweet sixteen party with tigers present, he saw how they were treated and wanted to do something. So he traded in his naughty ways at twenty-five, learned everything he needed, and opened up the rescue a few months later. He'd been helping animals ever since. A higher purpose in life.

My story wasn't as glorified as his. I was a cute little girl, I only had one sibling, parents divorced. Fell in love with pretty dresses and makeup at twelve. Have been best friends with Rayne forever, she's really like my family. I went to school for cosmetology, worked my ass off until I opened my own super awesome salon. He was a bit of a player, but with his money, good looks, and attitude, who could blame him? But since he started the rescue, there hadn't really been anyone.

He was too focused on the animals.

I wanted to cut a bitch when he said that most of the women wanted him for who he was and the money he had. Once they realized he was just a laid-back guy that made the rescue his priority, they didn't want him anymore. Yep, I was feeling pretty stabby after that.

I hadn't been with anyone since my ex, just because I felt like I was missing something. Turns out it was a sexy man who lived and breathed rescuing animals. Who would have believed it?

"Tomorrow's the last day of our bet." I felt like it was bearing down on us, and I didn't really know what to make of it. Would I go back to my life? Would I stay here? What would become of us? I felt like I needed something from this. A path to follow, some sort of reassurance.

"That it is." He held me close but didn't say anything else. I wasn't ready to drop it, so I kept talking.

"What are we going to do? I mean, we live quite a ways from each other. I have my salon, you have the rescue. When are we going to see each other?" I pulled back and looked him in his beautiful blue eyes. I wanted to make this work with him. I mean, hell, Cammy Jennings didn't tell just anyone that she loved them!

"We will work it out. Both of us are the boss, we can be a little more flexible than some." It wasn't the answer I was looking for, but I wasn't expecting him to ask me to marry him either. Feelings of doubt and the unknown hit me. I hadn't known Jake for long, and I was undoubtedly in love with him, but where did we go from there? I had to go back to my life. I had a business, and apartment. Jake couldn't have me around distracting him, driving off to have sex in the woods.

"Sweetheart. Look at me." I was staring at his chest. I didn't even realize I had looked away from his eyes. I returned my eyes to his.

"You love me?"
"Yes." I nodded.

"Then don't worry, any relationship has its kinks. We will work it out. We want it bad enough that there is no other way. I already told you. You're it." My heart swelled and I leaned in to kiss him. I had to believe that things would be okay. I had to.

"Okay, kitten." I called him the nickname I gave him in the beginning, to lighten the mood.

"I'll show you a kitten," he growled and mauled my neck. Teasing, licking, and nibbling.

"Knock, knock!" someone sang out by the door. Who the hell? I hopped off Jake so he could go to the door. Yikes, I totally forgot that this house was right dab in the middle of this rescue. Anyone could see us through a window. I needed to be more careful about that, maybe head upstairs or get some pretty curtains.

When Jake opened the door, he gestured for our guest to come inside.

"Rayne!" I bounced up and ran to hug my preggy bestie. She and Arson were here.

"What are you guys doing here?" I beamed. They looked so cute with their matching black hair and green eyes. Oh, their baby was going to be a cutie.

"I hadn't heard back from you today and wanted to check in on you, plus this place sounded cool. Jake said we could come by anytime, so I thought now was as good as any." She smiled while looking around. A crashing noise startled Rayne and me, as Casey jumped up onto the table to the right of us and then dashed off, Binksie slowly stalking her. They never stopped!

"Good lord." Rayne had a hand on her heart.

"Well, I'm glad you stopped by!" I hugged her again and gave Cammy Jr. a kiss.
"You're all right?" She gestured towards Jake.

"Oh yeah, I'm just dating a millionaire, but who cares, right? Although now that I think about it... you do know I have an addiction to shoes, right?" I gave him a wink and started chatting Rayne up about everything.

"Can we give them a tour?" I pleaded with Jake.

"Yeah, let me just put Casey in her crate for a nap. Don't want her tearing up the house while we're out." He had a point there. Not sure why some people thought owning a tiger would be fun. They destroyed everything. He walked off and grabbed the cub, placing her in her pen. She would be out in no time. Together, we all walked around, and I took the lead on the tour when I could. I was excited to share all the stuff I had learned. Everyone at the rescue knew everything already so I couldn't impress them.

"This is Koda, the bear. He's a retired circus bear. He had a pretty hard life, kept in a small cage, forced to do stunts, and travelling constantly. But he's pretty happy now. He likes to laze around his habitat and enjoy the fresh air." I pointed to the big bear that was hanging out in some water, enjoying the summer breeze. We kept walking. Rayne enjoyed seeing the wolves the most— something about her inner animal being a wolf.

I could think of myself as a house cat. I wasn't about to kill creatures to eat, I liked to be petted sometimes, and I loved naps. Yep, my inner animal was a house cat.

We walked around the rescue, saying hi to all the people and animals we passed.

Rayne cried a couple of times when hearing about some of the animals' stories. I didn't like it either. Humans were really terrible when it came to animals. One of the facts that Jake stated, and it hit me pretty hard, was that there were more tigers in backyards than in the wild. I hated people at that moment. Both Rayne and I were pretty upset about that, but we ventured on. The young lions we passed were rescues from cub petting, just like Casey, but instead of getting sick, they just got too big and were going to be "canned." Which meant they were going to be sold to the exotic hunting industry to be used in canned hunts where the hunter pays to hunt a fenced area for a guaranteed kill. Horrible. I just wanted to snatch all those animals that were still out there and bring them here, where they would be safe.

When we made it to the gift shop, I went straight to the kids' section and bought Cammy Jr. some cute animal outfits. Patty, the crazy lady at the desk, greeted me sweetly, and wrapped up the outfits for me.

"Okay, I think I'm good." Rayne plopped down so much stuff on the table, I was a little worried how she carried it all over.

"Rayne, good gracious!" She had picture frames, T-shirts, stuffed animals, a few packets to sponsor the animals, Skittles, and a wolf snow globe.

"I felt compelled, don't judge me." I saw Arson chatting with Jake off to the side, and gave my attention back to the mess in front of me.

"Oh and I'd like to donate, as well." Rayne smiled.

"Okay, dear, how much would you like to donate? I see you grabbed a couple of the animal sponsors. How would you like to split that up?" She held out four animal sheets. I stared at them. Those were not cheap sheets.

"A thousand for each, please." My eyes bugged out of my head at her answer. Holy shit, she was donating four thousand dollars! Plus everything she was buying in front of me.

"Holy hell, Rayne." I was stunned.

"I have to help somehow. This is all I can do." She looked at me and I saw the need to help in her eyes. After hearing all she had today, her heartstrings had officially been pulled. She wanted to give a new life to the poor creatures that had been mistreated for most of their lives.

"Thank you."

I didn't need to say anything else to her. What she was doing was amazing. As we said goodbye to my friends, I started thinking about things I could do to help. Maybe I could do a Wild Rescue day at the salon, with half off services, and donate the money to the rescue. Or maybe T-shirts or something. I wanted to help. This place was like my second home now. I felt it in my bones.

Chapter Twenty-five

'

I was pretty damn tired by the time I hit the hay. Jake had to run and check on the bobcat with the arrow wound, but promised he would be back shortly. I hoped that when he got back we could play hide the snake. And by snake I meant his penis.

I played with Binksie and Casey, letting them chase a laser light. Jake said that they loved to chase, and it was good for them. Made them use their physical and mental abilities. It just made me laugh. I fed the cats and made sure they used the litter. Casey wouldn't have a litter pan once she was in her habitat, but it helped for now. After they were tuckered out, we sat on the couch and they both snuggled against me on the couch. I grabbed my phone and was reading a hot romance when Jake walked in the house an hour later and put Casey in her crate.

"Let's go take a shower." He held his hand out to me and helped hoist me up. Binksie wasn't happy about me moving him to get up, but he sauntered over to his bed and flopped down.

"He's so comfy," I commented. Jake looked at the serval and nodded.

"He's a pain in the ass, too. They don't make good pets, but he gets too stressed being outside the house." Yeah, Binksie probably would be better out in the wild. Although after the high life he lives now, he would totally not survive. Spoiled cat.

"Shower, sweetheart." I looked up at him and nodded. He pulled me up so we could walk up the stairs. A question rolling through my mind while we walked was, would we be getting dirty in the shower at all? I hoped so. I could use some good cock pounding.

"Cock pounding?" Jake choked and looked at me. Oh God, I said that part out loud didn't I? Kill me now. Well, no going back now, I had to own it.

"Yep, I was just thinking how I could use some good cock pounding. Know anyone up for the job?" I walked into the bathroom and turned on the shower. I could feel the fuck me vibes coming from the silent man standing behind me now. It was buzzing over my skin, lighting the fires within.

"I might know a guy." His voice was husky and low. So hot. I think I needed some dirty talk from him. Jake was wild and I was one hundred percent in love with that. I didn't want the tame and reserved sex. I wanted the can't control anything, teeth clashing, back scratching, body slamming fuck. What we did last night was amazing, sweet and slow, and perfect. Every girl needs that every once in a while. But right now? Nope. Nada.

I peeled out of my clothes and looked behind me to see his eyes were zeroing in on my ass. I did a little wiggle and purred.

"Would you mind going and getting him, then?" I loved our banter. We both were playing a game, obviously not taking each other seriously. It was fun.

"I'll get on that. Until he gets here, mind if I fill you?" He took a step closer and shrugged his shirt off. Fill me? Uh, hells to the yeah! I scanned over his tan chest and down his sculpted abs to that sweet V I was going to lick. I moved my eyes back up to his.

"You'll do." I winked and jumped into the water. I didn't have to wait long until his body joined mine under the water's spray. Thank God for his large shower, otherwise this would have been a little snug.

"Vixen," he whispered against my ear. Shivers down my body? Check.

My nipples hardened just before his hands cupped them, kneading me softly. Nothing like someone rubbing your boobs to make all the stress in your life melt away. I arched into him, enjoying his attention. But after a few more seconds of his slow teasing moves, I craved the heat. I turned in his arms and my hand went straight for his erect cock. Yeah, I was going gung ho right now. I caressed him, running my thumb over the head gently.

A hiss came up his throat; his eyes closed briefly from the pleasure. Then they opened, and I had accomplished what I wanted to do— I unleashed the beast. My body hummed with excitement about what was about to go down. Poke the beast a little, and he would attack. A sexy, out of the world orgasmic attack was in my very near future. His lips crashed against mine as I was pressed up against the glass behind me.

His hands wrapped around the back of my thighs, lifting me up and right onto his cock. I was so ready for him, and he knew it. My head rolled back onto the glass. Heaven.

"You're mine, sweetheart. Full of my cock, this pussy knows who it belongs to. No one else can give you what I can," he gritted out through clenched teeth. I ground myself against him, needing him to move.

"I'm yours," I groaned.

"Want me to move, sweetheart? Fuck your sweet heat?" I nodded with my lip between my teeth. I so wanted that.

"Touch your tits, play with those rosy pink tips. I know you like that," he ordered and started to lift my hips, then bring me back onto him. I did as he said and pinched my nips, kneading them. I loved playing with my boobs.

"Best tits I've ever seen." His hips started pounding me against the glass. I hoped it didn't break from the forced of being nailed to it. With every thrust, I was getting closer and closer. Jake was true to his words and had been ever since I met him. He knew exactly what I wanted and needed. He was my alpha. My hands gripped his shoulders, nails biting into his skin. His mouth went straight for my neck, ravishing me.

"I..." I tried to form the words to let him know I was close but they didn't come out.

"I know, you're clenching me, beginning to quiver around my cock. Your soft walls are begging me to push you over the edge. Make you fall. Hard." His words ran along the lines of my neck, through my ears, and straight down to my core. I was so done for.

"That's right, sweetheart." He switched up his pace to slow and hard. Every time he pushed back in, his pelvis ground against my clit.

I shattered.

I had been close but that little move took me there in seconds, with Jake on my heels. He bit my neck and growled, something I would be looking forward to every time we came together like this.

"I love you." My head rolled forward to look at him.

"I love you." He lifted me up and off him, gently setting me down. I felt something running down my leg and was struck with a thought.

"We didn't use any condoms the past couple times." I looked into his eyes and saw nothing. No panic, just nothing.

"Okay," he shrugged, grabbing the bar of soap like it wasn't a big deal.

"What if I have herpes?" I mean, honestly. He gave me the look that called bullshit. Granted, he had been on a first name basis with my lady bits for a few days now.

"Then I guess we need to get married. We can be one happy herpes family," he smiled, teasing me. I shook my head. I was staring at him like he was crazy. He decided to finally take my stare seriously, and started rubbing the soap over his body.

"You clean?" he asked.

"Yes." No hesitation in my answer.

"You on birth control?"

"Of course." Once again, no delay on my answer.

"Then we have nothing to stress over. I'm clean, you're clean. No babies anytime soon, although I would like to see you grow with my child inside you. But there's no rush." My mouth dropped and he kept on washing himself. Once he was done, he looked me over and saw I was still in my shocked state. Taking initiative, he poured some of my body wash in his hands and started cleaning my body.

Not one to fight about getting washed by a sexy man, I let him continue doing what he was doing. I took the opportunity to stare at him and run his words over through my head. He wants to have a baby with me. Dear Lord. Something about the way he said it made me want to jump back on him and ride him until it happened. I wanted a family and my clock was ticking, but I didn't think I wanted it that soon.

After we were clean, dried, and dressed, we curled into bed.

"Because I know you've been going crazy in that head of yours over what I said, remember the part where I said no rush. We have all the time in the world, sweetheart. I still need to convince you to move in with me, take my name, and then we can work on babies." I didn't know what to think about that statement. It both frightened me and excited me. I wanted to tell him that I was moving in with him tomorrow, never going back, that we could get married and start that life. But I wasn't ready for all of that just yet. I wanted it, but I needed a wee bit more time to wrap my head around it. I gave him a kiss, and then snuggled against his naked chest. I listened to his heartbeat and lulled myself to sleep. I didn't want to think anymore, so dreaming was my next option.

I woke up in the middle of the night when Jake was getting back into bed.

"Sorry, go back to sleep. I just had to check on Casey," he whispered and pulled me close. I tried to go back to sleep but my bladder started screaming at me.

"I have to pee." I rolled out of the bed and padded over to the bathroom. It was dark, and I didn't want to turn on the lights to blind my eyes, but thankfully, I could still somewhat see where the toilet was. I pulled down my shorts and sat down. I heard a splash in the water beneath me, which, had I not been still very sleepy, would have clued me in that something was up. Instead I just sat there, trying to figure out what made that noise, and then something smacked into my ass.

I screamed.

I screamed my head off.

Falling off the toilet, I scrambled away with my bare ass hanging out, tearing out of the bathroom as fast as I could.

"What's wrong?" Jake was up and helping me get off the floor.

"Something just smacked my ass in the toilet!!" I screamed. I was assaulted, for Christ's sake.

"Oh shit, it was probably a toilet frog." Jake held me, rubbing my back while my shorts were around my ankles.

"What the fuck is a toilet frog?" My voice was starting to return to its normal octave. I felt a little chuckle escape his lips but I managed to refrain from smacking him.

"Every once in a while, a frog will get in through the vent and hang out in the toilet, like it's his own personal pool. Never bothered me. It's gone by now, if you still need to go." He was holding back more laughter. I untangled myself from him, and pulled up my shorts.

I didn't answer him. Instead, I walked out of the bedroom and to the other bathroom and did my business. After checking for creatures in the toilet. I was tired, and feeling a little pissy, so when I made it back to the bed, I stretched out and went back to sleep, not caring if Jake was still laughing or trying to cuddle me. I needed my sleep.

Chapter Twenty-six

The next time I woke up it was to the ringing of my phone. Nonstop ringing.

"Somebody better be dead," I grumbled and answered it, saying exactly that.

"Cammy, it's Mary. We have a situation at the salon. Someone spray-painted the word 'whore' on the door. It's bright red and huge." I jackknifed up and screamed.

"Are you fucking kidding me?" I was livid. Someone defaced my baby. Looking over at the clock, which said it was 7:30 a.m., I knew I had to get over there to handle it.

"It's crazy. What do we need to do?" She was panicking. I took a few calm breaths and spoke.

"I'll be there shortly. We'll find someone to get it cleaned off stat, and I'll check through the security cameras to find out who did it. For now, just open the door and make it look like we are letting some of the morning air in for any people walking by. Act like everything is normal. I'll see you soon." I hung up and jumped into action. I got dressed in a blue sundress, threw on some light makeup and put some mousse in my hair. I would be rocking the "bed head but works" look today. I grabbed my purse and put on some cute wedges to complete my look.

I found Jake downstairs finishing up breakfast, with Casey playing around his feet.

"I have to go. There's been some vandalism at my salon," I huffed. This was so not how I wanted to spend my day. Especially my last day at the rescue. Now it was back to reality.

"Vandalism?" He looked at me with shock. Yeah, tell me about it.

"Yep, someone spray-painted the word 'whore' on the door. Bright red. I have to go take care of it. Not sure when I'll be done." I kind of felt like this was farewell to the rescue. Not forever, but I wasn't sure when I would be able to come back. I had a business to run.

"Okay, I'll take you over since Bambi is at Rayne's. If you need anything, give me a call. Don't worry, sweetheart. We're big kids, we've got this." He walked over to give me one hell of a toe-curling kiss, then let me go. I gave him a smile and bent down to scratch Casey behind the ears. Her paw came out to get my hand but I yanked back before she could get me. Stinker.

With my purse in my hand, Jake drove me to my side of the world, and dropped me off with a sweet kiss. I so didn't want to adult today.

Hours later, the paint was off my door. Business was still going strong and no one had any issues. I looked over the cameras that were outside the door but whoever did it was covered in all black, like a ninja. Couldn't tell anything. I filed a police report and gave them what I could, which was pretty much nothing. And with me now dating one of the hottest eligible bachelors in the city, I was probably going to have a bunch of jealous bitches out to get me.

Which sucked, but, oh well. I wasn't giving him up because of this. I would fight on. I spent the day holed up in my office, going over things that I had missed from being away for a week. Nothing important. Papers to sign, plans to review, orders to confirm, payrolls to check, the life of a business owner. I was tired, and my girls were constantly coming in to check on me, but my mind was just racing. By the time I looked at the clock, it was almost six.

The salon would be closing soon, so I left the office and helped the girls close up. Rayne had brought me Bambi at some point so I could get back to my apartment without needing to call anyone.

As soon as I stepped foot in my home, I felt like I was in a stranger's apartment. I sat down on my pretty brown couch and called Jake.

"Sweetheart," he answered, which made me smile.

"I've had a day from hell," I groaned.

"I know a few ways I could make it better." I could see his smirk in my head.

"I know you could," I confirmed, but I didn't want to drive all the way out to the rescue right now, then come back in the morning. I was just too mentally wiped out.

"It'll be all right. I want to go take a bath, though. Call you later?" I was not in the socializing mood. I just wanted to take a bath and curl up in bed. Preferably with Jake, but that wasn't happening tonight.

"Of course."

"I love you." I stood up and walked into my bathroom.

"Love you, sweetheart." I sighed from the feeling in my chest. Him loving me was amazing.

"Talk to you later." We said goodbye and I got the makings for my bath.

The bath was wonderful, as expected. My sweet pomegranate bubbles surrounded me while I sat there and tried to empty my mind. When I say I tried, I meant I tried for five minutes. My mind kept wandering back to Jake, Casey, and the rescue. Suddenly my bath just didn't feel as good, so I hopped out and dried off. Once I was in my unicorn onesie that I reserved for bad days, I made myself a sandwich and sat on the couch. Alone.

I missed the sounds of the rescue. The lions roaring, the wolves howling. I missed it all. I looked around my apartment, feeling alone like never before. I couldn't have imagined that in just a week, my life would take such a huge turn. But it did. I wished I could do so many things to help the rescue.

Light bulb!

I got so excited thinking about the idea that just hit me. I could organize a block fundraiser on St.Armand's. All the businesses were pretty cool. I could host a get-together, get the community involved. Do discounted services and accept donations. My mind started running through all the things I could do, and before I knew it, I was calling Jake to let him know my idea. Which he approved of. He told me I would need to do a couple of things first, but otherwise he would help. He would bring all kinds of merchandise. We could totally set up some stuff in the middle of the circle where there was a pretty grass area with statues. After I was done talking over everything with Jake, I turned on Netflix and settled into bed. I had something to look forward to and I was excited. It was like I had a purpose for something bigger than myself.

Three weeks had passed since our week on the rescue and I was a busy bee. I'd been to Jake's every two days to stay the night. We'd spend our time in an orgasmic coma, making up for the lost nights together. I was also there when they moved Casey to her own little habitat. She was so happy to be free to run around, and pretend hunt in her own space. I would sometimes stop over to just talk to her, let her know how things were coming, and that the big fundraiser was going to happen soon. I made her fun little enrichment toys to play with as well; she liked those.

I was also able to take part in the release of the arrow bobcat back into the wild. The poor thing was nervous and scared to turn its back to us, but once we kind of hid in the shade it took off. Hopefully to live a happy life, arrow free.

All in all, my life was pretty good. Jake kept asking me to move out of my apartment and live with him at the rescue, but I wasn't quite there yet. Yes, my apartment was lonely and I missed them. But I wasn't ready to leave that life. Driving back and forth to my salon from the rescue every day would get old, and for now I didn't know what to do about that. I loved my salon, but maybe I was starting to want more in my life than that. I tried not to think of it too much as I got to work for the big block shindig.

Chapter Twenty-seven

Most of the businesses were excited to participate, and were offering up all sorts of goods in an auction, as well as willing to donate a percentage of their profits. I had face painters ready to go, and Autumn and Helen brought over a truckload of goods to sell. They were supposed to take a ton of pictures and live tweet from the party. We hadn't really gotten along any better since I claimed Jake in front of them, but today they were my bitches. Or minions, whichever you wanted to call them. People started filling up the streets, and in no time the fundraiser was a huge success. I walked through my salon and saw everyone was smiling and having a ball. I went into my office to grab a painting that Jake had sent with the girls. Casey had done it, and I was trying to figure out where I should put it.

"Cammy?" Mary's voice asked softly from my door. I turned towards her to see her glancing back out towards her hair station.

"What's up?" I inquired, setting the painting down.

"There's a chick here who keeps asking about you. She's being all shady." My feet swiftly moved over to where she was and peeked out to her spot. I wanted to laugh at what I saw.

Marlene Debarue. That little skank.

She was sitting in the chair in a black designer trench coat, and black sunglasses on. I would recognize her hair and facial structure anywhere.

"What has she been asking?" I was curious as hell. Jake warned her to stay away from me. She obviously wasn't ready to give up, but was trying to sneak around in her little disguise.

"She asked if this was Cammy's salon. If you were dating Jake, and did I like my job. I told her yes to the first one and excused myself to the bathroom. She is wanting a conditioning treatment to help bring out the shine in her blonde hair, and will probably keep digging. What do you want me to do?"

If I had an evil laugh, I would be doing it right now.

"I got this, Mary. Just get her a cooling eye pillow. I'm taking over after that." I smiled mischievously. You did not fuck with Cammy Jennings. And Marlene was about to figure that out.

"Poor girl," Mary muttered, but did as she was told. I knew what I had in mind was naughty, but honestly, she couldn't do shit. Especially after today, I was the community's sweetheart. Plus, I wasn't afraid of her. I watched as Mary got Marlene a cooling eye pillow on her face and got her wrapped up for a treatment. The pillow would help with those bags under her eyes. Man, I was a bitch.

Moving quietly over to their station, I prepared my tools; while I listened to her ask questions about me. I motioned for Mary to scoot out of there and I took over, changing my voice to sound similar to Mary's.

"So you do like your job then?" Marlene prodded. I dipped the brush into the liquid in the cup and started coating her hair.

"Well, between you and me, Cammy can be quite the slave driver sometimes." I was so going to enjoy this.

For the next twenty minutes, I continued to talk shit about myself to Marlene, who I was pretty positive was trying to find dirt on me to blackmail me in some way so I would leave Jake. As if. I had her sit under the heat for another ten minutes and finally washed all the caked-on crud out of her hair. After rinsing, drying, and doing a really beautiful style on her. It was time for the reveal.

"Your hair is so gorgeous. The shine is so perfect." I took a step back and took her eye pillow off for the big reveal.

Her ear-piercing scream made my insides all giddy. Payback was a bitch.

"Oh my God, what have you done?" she shrieked and finally looked at me. I smirked at her.

"I think you look great. I think it brings out the jealous snake that is on the inside. Green is definitely your color." Oh yeah, I totally went there.

"You are dead," she seethed. I just rolled my eyes.

"Whatever you're thinking of doing, just stop that little thought right there. This is over. You are done, leave. You know you can't touch me, and you know you don't want to fuck with Jake, either. Stop acting like a spoiled bitch whose favorite toy belongs to someone else. Move on. Oh, and because I am not a complete bitch and I do think you have nice hair, the green will wash out in a week. But now you know not to fuck with me."

A few of my girls yelled out, "That's right, girl," and "uh huh!"

Marlene looked around and I saw that she knew what I said was true. She was a brat, and there wasn't anything she could do. She screamed in frustration before grabbing her sunglasses and stomping out the door. Good riddance. A couple of the people who were in earshot of us started clapping at her departure.

"Back to the party, people!" I hooted and cleaned up the mess at Mary's station.

Everyone loved the fundraiser and when Jake showed up for a few minutes, I couldn't help but run into his arms and kiss the shit out of him. This was a magical day, and I was having a blast. Someone snapped a picture while we were lip-locked, but I didn't care. Hell, they could put us in the newspaper. I gave no fucks about it.

The party went on until 5p.m. and when it was all said and done, we had raised almost forty-five thousand dollars. We had a few large donations, and the auction was a hit. I was blown away by everyone's generosity and willingness to help. It really said something about how everyone really can come together to do good in the world.

Once everything was cleaned up, and the salon was shut down, Jake and I went out for pizza.

"I am starving!" I groaned, while taking a bite. I hadn't really eaten all day. It had been crazy, and I just didn't think about it.

"It's been a while since I ate pizza," Jake commented.

"Well if I ever move in, you'll just have to get used to it because pizza is a staple in my life." True story, bro. He didn't say anything to that comment. He wanted me to move in, but he knew I knew his opinion on the matter and he knew mine. No sense in battling it out now, especially not after the great day we had.

"Casey hasn't been feeling well today." I stopped eating and looked at him. She wasn't feeling well?

"What's wrong?"

"Looks to be just a cold. We are keeping a close eye on her though. With her compromised immune system, things could escalate quickly, but Doc thinks she'll get over it soon." I heard what he said, but I was still worried. From the moment I laid eyes on that baby tiger, she had captured my heart. I'd hate to see her sick. Poor girl.

"Okay, I think I'm going to stay on the rescue to help out until she gets better. Anything I can do." I wanted to be there. I hated it when I was sick, so I bet she wasn't too happy either.

"Sounds good." We went back to eating our food, then drove to the rescue. I already had clothes and my cosmetics in his house, so I didn't need to grab anything. Once we were parked, I headed straight to Casey's habitat. She was running around, but I heard a sneeze here and there. She looked fine, so it eased my nerves. Jake joined me shortly, carrying some chairs with him, so we could sit near her and chat. It was nice. I told both her and Jake about the fundraiser, and how amazing it was. I told him about Marlene, which he got mad about at first, until I told him about dyeing her hair green. It wasn't permanent, so I didn't care. She totally deserved it. Hannah came and checked Casey out and said she was okay, and told us to go get some rest. I wanted to watch her and make sure she did all right throughout the night, but I knew she would be fine. No one died of colds. Except aliens who weren't used to our bacteria, but she was no alien.

Chapter Twenty-eight

Together we took a shower, surprisingly with no heated touches, and then climbed into bed. As I laid there curled up in Jakes arms, my mind started turning dirty. He was just too much man to let a night go by without a romp in the sheets.

I kissed the warm skin that I was lying on and kept on moving. His hands started caressing my curves and the fire between us was lit.

We clashed, and together we burned in a beautiful fire. I was in control this time. Well, he let me be in control until I rode him into orgasmic oblivion, then he took over until he caught his own release.

The air smelled of sex and sweat, and my life had never seemed better.

Until Jake woke me up at 3 a.m.

"Sweetheart. You need to wake up." His voice was serious, but I still didn't move.

"Casey's not doing so good." My eyes flew open. I sat up and looked him over. His hair was a mess from him running his hands through it. Things were not good. Without a word, I threw on some clothes and we hopped on the ATV, heading toward Doc's house.

When I saw the sweet tiger lying in a crate, with IVs attached to her little legs, I started crying.

"I thought she was fine. She looked fine," I cried out to them as quietly as I could. I walked over to her crate and sat down on the ground next to her. Poor baby.

"She has pneumonia. There is fluid building in her lungs. We are giving her antibiotics, and a light sedative to keep her calm. There is hope that she will pull through." Hannah gave me a weak smile, one that said they hoped she would be okay, but that there was also a chance that she wouldn't. Only time would tell. I sat next to the sweet cub and started softly singing songs about being strong and fighting. She would be fine. Jake was silent as he watched me sing to her. He knew how much she had come to mean to me.

As the hours passed, and light started peeking through the windows, my hope started to build that she was going to be okay. I had barely moved throughout the night— once to go to the bathroom, and once more to get fresh air for a moment. Jake stayed by my side, and Hannah and Dr. Nick kept checking her vitals and IV. She was stable, for now.

"You two need to get some fresh air. She will be fine for now." Hannah was trying to get us to move. I didn't want to. I wanted to be there, but I knew I wasn't doing her any good. I was just taking up space right now. I needed to make myself useful somehow.

"Please keep us updated," I told her, and stood. My legs were sore from sitting on the tiled floor for so long, but it was a welcomed ache. Jake joined me and together we left the house.

"If you just want to rest at the lodge you can." He commented and I stopped him from speaking further.

"No, I need to do something. Keep my mind busy." He looked me over and wrapped me in his arms.

"I know this is tough. Many animals we rescue have been through so much that it's hard to see them go through anymore. You're strong, sweetheart. It'll be all right." He kissed my lips softly, and then hugged me tightly. I understood what he said, but I didn't truly take it to heart. Wild Rescue was a safe haven for these animals, and if there was a higher power why would he punish those who had already suffered? It wasn't fair.

"Put me to work, Jake," I demanded. He pulled back and looked into my eyes. I was determined to be of use, and keep my mind busy. He nodded and we got back on the ATV. One by one, we helped the workers clean habitats and make the food buckets. My arms were aching, and my back was sore. I had worked harder than I ever had before. Jake disappeared to take care of something while I helped Derek with the small animal habitats. Not even the damn wallaby could get to me now.

"Cammy," Jake uttered my name behind me. I looked at him in confusion. He called me Cammy. Not sweetheart.

"Come here." He held out his hand for me and I could tell something was wrong.

"Jake," I warned, not wanting to hear what he had to say.

"Come here," he demanded, and I went to him, my eyes pleading with him to just spit it out.

"Casey's not doing any better. She's suffering. We have to help her out of her misery." When his words finally registered, I took a step back, like I'd been burned by the touch of his hand.

"What?" my voice was so soft. Barely above a whisper.

"She isn't going to make it. The pneumonia is too much for her already weak immune system. We need to end her suffering." He pleaded with me to understand, but I just shook my head. No. No,no,no,no. I did the only thing I could think of— I ran to the house. Breathless, I opened the door to see Casey up on the surgery table, lying on a pink blanket. One IV was still in her leg.

I ignored the looks of Hannah and Nick as I walked over to the cub. I stroked her soft fur, and the tears flooded over my cheeks.

"You can't give up. You have to fight," I whispered to the cub. She was a fighter.

"Cammy, she's suffering. We have to help her," Hannah spoke, her voice laced with sadness but resolve.

"She can do this," I told her. She had to. I felt a strong hand on my shoulder, trying to comfort me. But I was already going under.

"No, Cammy, she can't. The fluid buildup in her lungs is too much and too rapid. She's practically drowning. We need to end her pain now. We'll let you say goodbye, then we have to end it. It's the humane thing to do." Her voice was strong; it wasn't easy to do what she had to do. And somewhere in the back of my mind, I knew it was the right thing to do. The tears kept coming as I heard steps go into the other room.

"I'm so sorry for everything, Casey. So sorry for those evil people that took you from your mother. That set this fate into motion. They forced you to be a prop for their own greed and selfish needs. They made it so you never really had a chance. You escaped one death only to be taken by another." I was crying my heart out to the sweet girl.

"I'm glad I got to see you enjoy your life for those few weeks. I hope there is a tiger heaven with lots of land, and things for you to chase. You'd like that." I sniffed.

"I'm so sorry, Casey," I apologized, weeping. Hoping somewhere in there, it would register what I was saying. I wished things were different. I touched her fur one last time. My eyes closed, and I whispered the words that I never wanted to say.

"Goodbye, sweet cub."

I stood there and watched as the doctors came back into the room and put a syringe into the IV tubing and pressed the medicine through the line. I watched as her chest wheezed and, finally, she took her last breath.

I crumpled to the floor. My heart was broken. The only animal I had ever loved had been taken. It was like someone had ripped a hole in my chest. I sobbed and Jake scooped me into his arms, taking me away from the lifeless little striped body on the table. My wails of a painful heart could be heard throughout the rescue as he took me back to the lodge. I couldn't move; I couldn't breathe. Why did this happen? She had suffered enough in her little life. She was supposed to grow big and strong.

I cried in Jake's arms on the couch for what seemed like hours. I was devastated.

He didn't say anything to me. He simply held me. I'm sure he'd been through this many times, but I hadn't. I didn't want to feel like this ever again. My mind turned dark as I started drowning in the sadness of losing something so close to my heart. I sat up from Jake and started to stand. I had to get out of here. I had to leave this rescue. No one could escape death, not even those who had already suffered. I wasn't made to deal with this much emotion. My throat felt like it was closing and I was struggling to breath. I couldn't live my life dealing with constant suffering and pain. It just wasn't in me. I was safer in my old life, before the rescue. Before Jake.

"Cammy. What are you doing?" Jake was looking at me like he was scared to make a move. Scared to spook me. But he was too late. I was already spooked.

"I can't do this." The words flew from my lips on a whisper. The tears were coming back in full force when he realized what I had said. I was leaving. For good.

"You can. You're strong. We can make it through together, Cammy. Just give it time." He slowly got up and I took a step back, shaking my head. I wasn't strong enough for this heartbreak.

"I can't, Jake." He looked pained when I whispered the words again. I hated that I was hurting him. But I needed it all to end. The pain, the future heartbreak. I couldn't handle it. I'd rather be alone.

"I can't leave them, Cammy." He knew my mind was made, and we both knew this was the end. They needed him. This rescue needed him. He did so many wonderful things for them. But there was always a chance for things to go wrong. A chance I couldn't take anymore.

"I know." This was it. I couldn't look at his face...the devastation was clear. Taking a deep breath, I wiped the tears under my eyes and turned to gather my things. I heard the door slam as I started packing. I hated what I was doing to him. But I would hate myself even more if we moved in together, got married, had children, and then I broke. This life was not my life. I dragged my stuff out and packed Bambi. I didn't see Jake as I sat in my car and started the engine. I didn't blame him. I had shattered his heart and there was nothing he could do. This wasn't a life you could force someone to accept. I closed the door and saw him pull up on the ATV. Watching me.

I lifted a hand in a halfhearted farewell, and he gave me a head bow. Our final goodbye. I drove out of that rescue, leaving my broken heart on the porch surrounded by the sounds of the wild.

Chapter Twenty-nine

Once everything was back in my apartment, I grabbed the old bottle of Vodka in the back of my cabinet and started drinking. I wanted the pain to go away, even if just for a moment. I had just lost something that was precious to me. A future I hadn't even imagined I would have wanted. Now that future was shattered. I lay on my couch and let the sorrow take me into the darkness.

I woke up at my normal time, feeling like shit. My feet shuffled me into the bathroom to clean up, at least on the outside. I had a business to run, and even though I wanted to sit and sulk in my apartment, I couldn't.

I kept busy doing little things here and there, and at the end of the day I went back home. I ate until my body couldn't move and then watched TV. I was depressed, plain and simple. I would go through the cycle of emotions—

feeling horrible, then crying, then hating myself, then missing Jake. It had only been a day and I missed him so much I could barely breath. His smile, his witty banter with me, the way he cuddled me at night. Which made me go through another round of sobs, because I chose a life without him. Turned out I was right from the beginning. We didn't work.

A week went by in a blur of going through the motions, pigging out in front of the television, and crying buckets of tears. I guess my eyes were making up for all those years of never crying. You would have thought my ducts would have dried up or rusted by now. While I was finishing the episode of my new favorite TV show, *Lucifer*, someone knocked on my door.

Hope sprang inside me that it would be Jake on the other side, but I knew it wouldn't be. He couldn't choose me over his rescue, and I wouldn't want him to.

"Open up, Cammy." Rayne's voice filtered through the door. I looked around my apartment and sighed. It looked like shit. My luggage from staying at Jake's house was still by the door. Clothes littered the floor and there were food wrappers everywhere. I had never been this person, and I never wanted to be. But now that I was, I didn't care to change it. Wearing sweatpants and one of Jake's Henley shirts that I stole, I got up and opened the door.

"Oh dear God, what is that smell?" Rayne gagged. I took a shower this morning, so I knew it wasn't me, but maybe I had become nose blind to my apartment.

"Get out." She pulled me out of the apartment and closed the door behind her.

"What the hell, Rayne?" I complained. She took a couple breaths and sniffed the air in the complex hallway. Seeming satisfied with the smell, she looked at me and her eyes were wide as she took in my appearance.

"What's your middle name?" she blurted out frantically. She placed her hands on my shoulders and looked right into my eyes.

"Renee." I rolled my eyes.

"What is our favorite thing to eat together?" She kept up the inquisition.

"Pizza, Rayne. Why the hell are you asking me stupid questions in the hallway of my apartment?" I flailed out of her hold on my shoulders. I hadn't talked to her since she and Arson had come to visit the rescue, which now that I was thinking about it, was probably the reason why she was here. Which she confirmed.

"I hadn't heard from you since we were at the rescue, and your apartment stinks. My pregnancy nose can't handle it unless you want me to barf all over your living room." She pointed a finger at me, as if I was in trouble. I just shrugged.

"Cammy, what happened? This is not like you at all." Her face was full of concern. I wanted to vomit out the words but I wasn't ready yet.

"Remember when you cut things off with Arson, and I was there for you? No explanations, nothing? That's what I need. I don't want to talk about it right now. I want to sit on my couch, watch my show, and eat my Chinese food. I feel like shit, I'm on my period, and I'm an emotional wreck." I watched as her face turned from concern to sadness. She knew at least some of what I was feeling. Not all of it, but she had hit this point in her life when she was devastated, and all she could do was cry and go through the motions. Almost every night I stayed with her and was there for her. Her devastation ended when Arson fixed their problems. Mine couldn't be fixed. You couldn't make someone be somebody that they weren't.

"Ok, well, can you at least make your apartment smell a little better and I will be there for you, like you were for me?" She gave me those puppy dog eyes and I huffed a bit, but when I went back into my apartment, I threw away some food wrappers, opened a window and lit some candles. Hopefully that would help. I didn't want her to be sick. She came into my apartment, but didn't barf right away, so we figured she no longer would need a hazmat suit.

Together we watched more episodes of *Lucifer*, and pigged out together. She was pregnant, and I was depressed. Together we were the devourers of food. She spent the night with me, but had to leave in the morning to meet Arson for breakfast. I knew how I was acting was unhealthy, but I couldn't get out of it.

Another week passed and I was starting to feel a tiny bit better. I didn't cry every night for hours. Maybe only like two.

"We are going out tonight, no buts. I'll drag you out by your red hair if I have to." Mary barged into my office. I looked at her and nodded. I could go out. Maybe it would be good for me. She looked taken aback that I agreed to go, but then pointed her finger at me with a serious expression on her face.

"Get your ass in my chair, we are going to pamper you up, then you're going to go home, put on a pretty dress and stellar heels. I will have Rayne pick you up at eight. We've got five hours. Move it!" She was like a parent yelling at her child. Hitler mommy. Having no fight in me, I turned off my computer that I was just staring at anyway, and sat in her chair. She gave me a light trim, and wrapped my hair up high. I was then pushed into one of the massage rooms, given a treatment which was sort of painful since I was so tense, but it still felt good. Then I was given a pedi and mani. Red polish. A powerful color. They were trying to get me to buck up. Mary put me back in her chair and began to style my hair straight. My hair always looked so long this way, but I hadn't had the time prior to my auto pilot like state to work it.

"Get home. Rayne will be there to get you in a bit." I felt like a sheep being herded by a dog. I was never truly one to take orders; only Jake could make me do things like that. It made me feel worse that I wasn't myself. I wanted to change, I wanted to forget the pain of losing Casey, and giving up Jake. As soon as I got home, I really tried hard to bring back the happy, spirited Cammy that I always saw in the mirror. But I failed. A part of me was broken, and until I was put back together, I wouldn't be the same woman. Once I finished getting ready, I looked in the mirror and saw the Cammy everyone else knew. They would have to be satisfied with that. Rayne knocked on my door a few moments later.

"Is it safe to come in? I'm feeling extra smell sensitive today." I opened the door, and tried to smile.

"The apartment is stank free." She walked in and took a whiff. I had cleaned up a bit, in my attempt to feel better.

"You look better, but are you actually doing better?" She looked me over but saw right through my put-together exterior. I shrugged.

"Not really. I'm broken and I don't see me being fixed anytime soon. Give me some time." It was the best answer I could give her. Time. Hopefully time would do as they say and heal all. We walked down to her car and she drove us to Jackie D's. As we pulled in the parking lot, I wanted to tell her to take me home. Asia got out of the car, I was reliving my memories with Jake, and how this all started. It was here that he threw down his intent to chase me and that he was my alpha. It was here that I sang karaoke to him and passed out, landing me at his house, and losing that stupid bet.

Both Mary and Rayne tried to get me to cheer up, but being here was beginning to be too much. "I need some air. Alone," I told them, and started walking out the back towards the beach. Taking my shoes off, I walked to the water's edge. There was no one around and I finally let a few tears fall that had been brimming in my eyes since I got to the bar. I sat on the sand, even in my pretty dress, and tried to calm myself. I needed to break free from this pain. I was hurting so much, and I didn't want the sorrow anymore. I felt someone behind me, and turned quickly. I may have been out of my mind but I didn't want to die on the beach because I wasn't paying attention. I had to squint a little to see whom the figure silhouetted by the bar's lights was, but when it registered, I felt like crying all over again.

Chapter Thirty

"Jake." His name was a whisper on my lips.

"Sweetheart." Hearing my nickname coming from his did me in, I cried. I felt his arms wrap around me and scoop me up against him. It felt so good to be in his arms. My hands touched him, and my tears soaked his shirt. He walked us over to a beach chair that was still in sight of the bar's lights, but not as bright.

"I've missed you so much." As my words came out, my lips were in search of his. I needed him, I needed him to take away the pain.

"Make me forget for just a moment. Please Jake." My hands started pulling at his belt. I was upset, but I still loved him and wanted him.

"Sweetheart, I need you back in my life." His lips found mind and that was the match to our fire. I didn't give him an answer. I couldn't be in his life, not in the way we both wanted. But we could have this moment.

"You have me. Right now." It was all I could do. Seeming okay with my answer, his hands slid to the hem of my dress and pushed it up. My fingers finished on his belt and made quick work of his zipper. With ease, he flipped us so I was beneath him, eagerly spreading my legs for him. I was ready, and needed him like nothing before. My tears had ceased and my mind was focused on one thing: no pain, no hurt, only Jake. His lips clashed with mine and he pushed my tiny panties to the side. We didn't have long enough to take our time. We both knew this was our moment, and that was it.

My back arched into him when he slid inside me, I cried out into his mouth, and felt at peace. He moved with long and hard strokes. Filling me over and over, like the waves as they constantly crashed onto the sand. His body pressed into mine and I wrapped my arms around him, needing the closeness. He was my everything, and yet he couldn't be anything to me. I shut off my mind and gave into the sensations of the man selflessly giving me himself, when he knew I couldn't give him what he wanted.

"Oh God... Jake..." I was close. He lifted my right leg and brought it up to his hip, giving him a deeper angle.

"That's right, sweetheart. Give me your release." He groaned into me as my pussy started to quiver. I was going to burst, and when his lips moved down my cheek and to my neck, I knew he was, too. The thought of him biting my neck while he came shot me straight into my release. My head rolled back as I silently screamed and the stars above us went black. When his teeth sunk into my shoulder, I knew I would never come back from him. I would never love another man, and I could never give my body or soul to anyone else. He was my mate.

"I love you, sweetheart." The tears threatened to come back but I fought them off. I may not have been fixed on the inside, but I did have an understanding with myself now. I would always love him, but I couldn't live in his life.

"I will always love you, Jake. Until the day I die, but it is still too much." He looked at me, understanding in his expression.

"You'll always be my mate, and I will be there for you. Whether we are together in this life, or the next." He slowly eased out of me and moved my panties back into place. I sat up while he stood, putting himself back in his pants and zipping them back up. Needing one last touch, I stood and wrapped my arms around him.

"I'll be there, sweetheart." I nodded at his words and leaned up to give him one last kiss. He made sure it was one I would never forget, searing the feel of his lips on mine like a brand. When the kiss broke, he walked me back to the bar and left. I hated seeing him go, but at least we parted this time both knowing where we were. The death of Casey wasn't so fresh and emotionally draining me. I was still affected, but I felt like for the first time in weeks, I could finally breathe. Rayne and Mary were on me as soon as I sat at the bar.

"We saw Jake come in, then disappear. You okay?" Rayne asked and I nodded.

"Yeah, I actually feel better." I gave her a halfhearted smile. They both accepted my answer and for the rest of the night, I tried to enjoy being out and alive. When we got back to my apartment that night, I didn't feel upset, or shed one single tear. I felt alone still, but I had been alone before Jake and would be all right being alone now. I showered, and changed into some jammies, then lay down in bed to read.

I checked on the rescue's Facebook page quite a bit as weeks passed since my beach sex with Jake. I smiled when I saw that the money I had helped raise went toward new fencing and a brand new enclosure for a bear they would be bringing in. Another retired circus bear. I doubt Koda and the new bear would be able to be around each other, but it was still nice that the money went to good use. Jake hadn't been in any videos lately. I knew this because I checked. Often.

I just wanted to see his face. But both Autumn and Helen had taken over that duty for now it seemed. Word of Casey's passing spread as well. While it made me very sad, it made me proud to see so many people comment, share, and spread awareness of cub petting. Maybe one day things could change and cub petting would stop. But, until then, the people who were aware were the cubs' voices. They had the knowledge to create change.

I busied myself with work, and trying to be a human again, all while helping Rayne with the nursery. They had decided to stay in the apartment for now, but had plans to move into a house near the water. We decorated the room in a sea creature theme. He or she was one super-loved baby. Helping Rayne had given me something to focus on, something I was starting to lack in the other facets of my life.

"Your body is so hot," I grumbled as Rayne laid under my covers. She was due any day now, and her body was like a furnace. Arson was working with some contractors at his gym all night and wouldn't be done until about noon, so I told her she could stay with me. Keep her company and be there if she needed anything.

"Sorry, I've been sweating like a pig at night now. This baby needs to be done cooking soon. I'm tired of not being in control of my body." She rolled her bigger belly towards me. I scrambled out of the comforter and lay on top of it. Much cooler.

"Try and get some sleep, babe. I'll be fine," I promised her. She needed her rest; Arson said she had been waking up in the middle of the night wide-awake lately, so I figured she must be exhausted. Her soft breaths let me know she had fallen asleep. Once I knew she was out and didn't need anything, I let myself finally drift off, until my phone beeped and woke me up at 5a.m. I grabbed my phone and read the text message. It was from my pharmacy, saying that my birth control was ready to be picked up. I read it a couple of times, trying to understand it. It wasn't time for me to get my birth control yet. I still had another week.

I flipped over to my calendar app and counted the days. And then counted them again. And again. Something wasn't right. I was supposed to pick up my birth control, and the week that was my off week, I didn't get my period. So it's been four weeks since I had my last period, Jake and I had sex in the middle, I didn't get Aunt Flo when I was supposed to. For some reason I kept trying to figure out which was wrong, the text or the calendar. As gently as I could, so I wouldn't wake Sleeping Beauty, I got up and went to look at my birth control pack. Which was actually difficult, because I couldn't remember where it was.

"Well, that isn't good." I looked all over in places I would have put the pack, and finally found it in my drawer in the bathroom. I really hoped I was a responsible adult and took my pills like I was supposed to. Slowly I opened the pack, treating it like a vicious animal. Half-empty.

"Crap," I muttered.

I stood there and chewed on my bottom lip, afraid to think of what this could mean. My mind was going crazy. I had to know, so I dug through my cabinet for the little box. Years ago I had a pregnancy scare with a boyfriend. Thankfully it was just a false alarm, but I still had one stick left. Once I found the box, I pulled out the foil-covered pee stick and stared at it. God, what if I was? I was terrified to find out.

"Put your big girl panties on, Cammy." I tried to give myself a pep talk. I took a couple breaths, sat on the toilet and peeled back the foil. I held the stick down below, ready to pee. But I couldn't make myself do it. I was beyond nervous about what I was thinking.

"Pee. It's okay. You wanted a family, so it's okay. We got this. Just pee." I was talking to myself, willing my body to just let it flow. As soon as I start to golden shower the stick, I heard Rayne call my name from the bedroom.

Chapter Thirty-one

"Just a minute," I yelled back.

"Cammy, I need you, like now," she yelled back and hearing the tone in her voice, I knew something was happening. I finished peeing, wiped, set the stick on the counter, washed up and ran out to her. She was sitting on my bed, staring between her legs where a big wet spot had emerged.

"Did you pee my bed?"

"I don't think so." She shook her head.

"Will you smell it?" she asked me in all seriousness. I backed away waving my hands frantically.

"Hell, no. You're the one with the freaky sense of smell, you smell it." Heck, no, I wasn't smelling that. She touched her stomach and winced. Wet bed forgotten for now.

"You okay?"

"I think I'm having a baby," she announced and I panicked.

"Oh crap, all right, we need to go! I'll get the bags, and whatever else. Are you hungry? Do you want some water? Um, crap, crap. Okay. I need to change. Uh, you should probably change, too. Oh, I will call Arson. He should probably know that his kid is on the way. Okay. We got this. Breathe. Everything is going to be just fine." I was pacing and breathing heavy. I looked at Rayne to see her still sitting on the bed, watching me and holding back laughing.

"How are you still sitting there? You are having a baby, for Christ's sake. Why aren't you up and moving? We need to get you to the hospital, like stat! Don't sneeze or cough either! I don't want any babies born in my apartment." With that, she finally burst into a fit of giggles. What part of having a baby did she think was funny?

"Oh, Cammy. The baby isn't going to just fall out of me. My vagina isn't a laundry shoot. This is my first kid; it's going to be a while. Hours, most likely. The contractions aren't bad. Let's just get ready. No rushing, then head to the hospital. Relax. Don't stress me, stressing will only make me worse." She smiled and shook her head.

I helped her up from the bed and together we got ready to leave. I called Arson on the way, and he said he would meet us at the hospital. Rayne's contractions were picking up, but she was breathing through them, my tough girl. Arson was at the door when we walked in and tried to get Rayne in a wheelchair but she refused. Something about walking helped move the baby down more. After signing some paperwork, they dressed her in an ugly blue hospital gown and set her up in a room. It was much different from what I was thinking a labor room would be. It was actually pretty nice.

Rayne had signed up for a room with a shower and a bathtub, aiming for a water birth, au natural. I cringed when I heard her say that, but to each her own. Rayne was a fighter and I had no doubt that if anyone could do it, she could.

We waited and held her hand when she needed it, until she was far enough along that she could get in the tub. On her knees, with her arms resting on the sides of the tub, she breathed through the painful contractions while Arson massaged her lower back. Man, what a team. The doctor came in and checked her to see how much she was dilated, and smiled.

"We are ready to start pushing," she announced. Rayne was covered in sweat, as she sat naked in the tub. I had officially seen every part of my best friend. Every part.

She had asked me to stay and I agreed. I was now in this until that baby popped out. Arson held one hand and I held the other, as she clenched her teeth and started to push. I watched as my bad ass Xena-like friend pushed, naturally, for thirty minutes, until a little baby boy was born.

"A boy," Arson whispered, looking at his child in awe. There was a full head of black hair on the baby's head, and he was big, too.

"Lie back, he needs skin to skin contact right away." Rayne did as she was told and they placed the tiny little thing on her chest. Tears were streaming down her cheeks from joy. Arson leaned over and kissed her head. I was elated for them, utterly happy for their new bundle of joy. As they cleaned Rayne up and Arson got to hold his son, I sat there, holding my best friend's hand in her moment of pure joy seeing her two boys together. Something clicked inside me. This was what I was missing.

Casey's passing was traumatic, and sad. But with every death came life. It was the way of the world. I was missing the happiness of love. The love of someone who adored you, even through your ups and your downs. The love of family, and the love of life. Right now Arson and Rayne were living their lives to the absolute fullest. They had everything they ever wanted right here in this room. I knew what I wanted and I needed to take a leap of faith. I knew there would be heartbreak in my life, but if I got to experience life like this, it would be worth it. I just needed to accept it and never look back. I had so much to give to this world, and I knew that with love by my side, I could do anything.

"Thanks for staying," Rayne whispered to me, and I squeezed her hand slightly.

"No other place I'd rather be." I smiled. Arson walked over to me and told me to hold out my arms. When he placed that sweet child in my arms, I was in love. He was so beautiful, and I told his parents as much.

"You guys have a name?" I asked, and brushed my hand over his soft hair. He squirmed but was otherwise calm.

"Cameron Leo Kade." Rayne smiled and my eyes flew to hers. Tears started sneaking out of my eyes, and finally, after so many weeks of grief, I was crying tears of happiness.

"Really?" I questioned excitedly.

"Yep. After his Auntie Cammy." She winked and that was all it took for me to take that leap of faith. This was life, this was happiness, and this was love. The ultimate goal in life.

I stayed until they got Rayne set up in the room she would be in overnight, then I left and went home with a smile on my face. I felt like the Cammy I was yesterday was gone. Banished to the depths of the universe. Once I got into my apartment, I packed a ton of clothes, and went into the bathroom for my makeup bag.

I stopped in the doorway and stared at the stick I had totally forgotten. Feeling resolved to be happy either way, I walked over and looked down at the results.

"Two lines," I smiled, and held it up closer to inspect.

"I'm pregnant." I hooted. I was pregnant and all I could think about was a little redheaded girl, raising hell just like her mother. I made sure the cap on the stick was tight and put it in my purse, then headed out the door. I left my bags, and everything behind and jumped into my car.

As safely as possible, I sped towards my life of happiness.

Chapter Thirty-two

I parked the car outside the lodge and ran inside.

"Jake!" I called out to see if he was here but heard no answer. Binksie looked up from his bed in the living room and if I knew he wouldn't scratch the hell out of me I would have hugged him. Instead, I settled for walking over and petting his head.

"I've missed you, boy." He started purring and leaning his head into my hand.

"I'll pet you more later, okay? Right now I need to find him," I told the cat and began thinking of where I could find Jake. He wasn't out by the pregnant Gemma, nor was he within sight. My gaze spotted the ATV and knew he must be walking around on foot. Feeling an opportunity here, I hopped onto the ATV and started searching. If he asked why I was driving it, I would just kiss him and shut him up.

My breath got stuck in my throat when I finally found him. He was helping build the new enclosure for the bear I had read about. When he heard the ATV pull up, he looked over with his hand shading his eyes, trying to see through the sunlight.

I stopped and hopped off, but didn't move. Neither did he. We just stood there, so many words in our locked gaze. However, one word hung in the air between us like a cord.

Forever.

Our forever wouldn't happen unless we were together. So I took off and ran towards him. He took a few steps and opened his arms, as I jumped into them, and wrapped my arms around him.

"I love you, Jake Wild. And I'm never leaving you again. You're my mate for life." I nestled in his neck, feeling him, and smelling him. Dirt, sweat and all.

"Mine forever." I could feel his grin against my head. Feeling like we needed to seal our promise with a kiss, I eased back and looked into his eyes. This right here was my missing piece. As our lips met with a promise of forever, my life clicked back into its rightful place. I enjoyed our kiss for a few moments, before the news I had burst out of me.

"Jake." I tried to pull back, but he wouldn't let me.

"Jake, I need to tell you something," I tried again, this time he let me pull back, but only enough so we could see each other's faces.

"I'm preggers." I beamed, watching his face for a reaction. Which I didn't get any. Not quite what I was hoping for, so I started back pedaling a bit.

"In my depressive state, I was an idiot, and forgot about my birth control pills. And as you know, we had sex on the beach, and well, being that you are a big alpha man, your sperm were all about making babies, so I really didn't have a choice in the matter. I..." He silenced me with a kiss, then groaned against my lips.

"You know when you rattle on like that, it turns me on like nothing else, sweetheart." I felt the evidence of that growing as he spoke.

"Right." I nodded.

"You're having my baby?" he purred against my lips. I liked it when he did this.

"Yep. You ready for two of me?" I teased.

"Lord help us all." I was about to go off on him for that response, but if I was being honest, he was right. Mini-me and I would rule the world. Our lips connected again, and with the sounds of the animals roaring in what I interpreted as approval, we jumped back into the pages of our beautiful story of love.

We spent the rest of the day helping with the new bear enclosure and our night wrapped in sheets, enjoying our new forever.

The morning sun woke us up. Yeah, Jake slept in with me. I was shocked to wake up with him still holding me in his arms.

"Rayne had the baby yesterday. I really want to go see them. Wanna go with?" I smiled, hoping that would help influence him to go with me.

"Sure." He kissed my forehead and I snuggled against him, enjoying this moment of waking up together. After another ten minutes of snuggling, I had the urge to pee so we decided it was time to get up. Jake checked in with Derek to make sure things were calm enough for him to sneak away for a few hours, and I cleaned up, and dressed myself in a cute green sundress. As soon as Jake finished checking in, we left in his truck and drove to the hospital—stopping for a bacon egg and cheese biscuit on the way, of course. Mimi-me needed breakfast.

Rayne and Arson were snuggling their sweet baby when we walked through the door.

"Hey, parental! How was the first night?" I plopped down on the couch, while Jake stood next to me.

"Pretty good. He ate through most of it, so not very much sleep for us. But he exhausted a lot of energy being born and all, he needed to fill up." Rayne smiled but you could tell she was tired.

"Fun stuff," I commented. I mentally crossed my fingers that our baby was a sleeper like me.

"So I see you guys are back together. Does this mean you told him?" Rayne was looking at me with a happy gleam in her eyes, while I had a gleam of confusion staring back at her.

"Huh?" I cocked my head to the side.

"That you're having his baby." She shook her head like it was ridiculous she had to answer that question. Arson choked and had to cough out his surprise.

"How did you know?" My voice was a little loud, but honestly, I was shocked she knew. She rolled her eyes.

"You left your stick on the counter in the bathroom. Not very discrete, babe." Well, there you go. I blushed a little, remembering how I had completely forgotten about the stick and freaked out about getting her to the hospital. Everyone in the room laughed. Which made little Cameron wake up. He squealed and Rayne took him to her breast to feed. Jake discretely averted his eyes and we all started chatting about babies, the rescue, and just enjoying life together.

At this moment, besides waiting to have our own little bundle of joy, I couldn't imagine life getting any better.

About a month had passed since I came back to the rescue, and man I had been so unbelievably busy. After much consideration, I had come to the conclusion that while I still loved my salon and everything that it entailed, it was no longer my passion.

Mary mentioned that she would love to buy it from me, and I agreed. Together we worked out a plan where she would rent to own with me. I taught her well and I knew she would do my baby right. It was hard to come to that final decision, but I knew it was the right one. I wanted this life. I wanted to be here on the rescue, making a difference and raising our child. One day while I was perusing through the gift shop looking at all the things I wanted to buy the baby, an idea hit me. An idea that was all me and was close to my heart, so I went back to the lodge and drew out my thoughts.

Three bananas, and one pee break later, I looked over my design.

It was a T-shirt with a tiger head on the front; underneath the tiger it said *I am their voice*. I was going to start a movement. On the back of the shirt it had #CaseysLegacy. I would tell Casey's story and create awareness to end cub petting. It was a start, and I wanted to do it. I would have the girls brand it, and we would have everyone tweeting, instagramming, and sharing the hashtag worldwide. Jake looked over my drawing later that night and thought it was a great Idea.

He was a happy man that I was here with him, in his life, a part of this mission to help the animals, and with his child growing rapidly in my belly. Before we fell asleep, we started talking about building a house back by the edge of the property, near the shed that housed his sexy beast of a car. I wanted a little more privacy, and a pool. We lived in Florida. I wanted a pool.

The next day I woke up to a note that told me to meet Jake out by the cheetah's enclosure. It was around 8:30 in the morning, and I figured I might as well get up. I dressed quickly and walked out to the habitat, but not before grabbing a granola bar on the way out. There was a camera guy set up again for another YouTube video, with Jake ready to be filmed. I noticed something green hanging from one of the trees and the cat was in its little nook.

"What's this video about?" I alerted everyone to my presence with a question. When Jake's eyes met mine, he smirked. Oh, that smirk. So hot and so infuriating at the same time.

"Piñatas," he finally answered. I looked over towards the green thing in the tree and noticed it was indeed a piñata. One in the shape of an M. Weird, but okay. I would have gone for a unicorn, personally.

"Ready to shoot?" the camera guy asked Jake, and he nodded. He made a quick joke about how the cats like piñatas and celebrating a special day. I ran through my mental list of holidays and came up with none for today. However, maybe it was a feline version of Cinch de Mayo or something. Or maybe someone's birthday? We walked around to all the enclosures that had the piñatas set up and I realized that they were all letters.

M.

A.

R.

R.

Y.

M.

As we watched the lion about to attack the last piñata of the day, something in my mind made me purse my lips. Why all the letters? I went through them in my head and took in the one that the lion had knocked down.

E. A fucking purple E.

Shock ran over my face and then I saw that the camera was no longer on the cat, but on me. Oh my God. I looked at Jake just as he took a step towards me, and bent down onto one knee. He reached into his pocket and pulled out the most beautiful ring I had ever seen.

"Cammy sweetheart Jennings, will you be the Nala to my Simba and marry me? Be my wife, my mate forever?" He smiled, obviously very proud of his little joke, but I laughed and lunged for him.

"Yes, you ridiculous man!" I kissed him and he slid the ring on my finger.

Our life was perfect. No wall we needed was to welcome our baby into the world and complete the puzzle in our perfect life.

** To date, the video of Jake proposing to me with the big cats' piñatas was on YouTube's top 100 most viewed videos of all time. *

Epilogue

Andrew Williams, a friend of Casey Wild

Sixteen years later

I wiped the sweat from my head as I pushed the lawn mower across the large front yard. I noticed Casey from the corner of my eye, heading toward me with a lemonade in her hand. I turned off the engine and smiled at her. She was a sweet girl, but a hellfire.

"Brought you some lemonade." She smiled and handed it over to me. I gulped it down like a man would in the desert. August in Florida felt like the desert.

"Thanks." I handed it back to her.

"When you're done, do you want to hang out in the pool for a bit?" She bit her bottom lip, and as tempting as that was, I was in love with someone else, and our classmate Cameron had warned everyone off trying to date this girl. Everyone except her could see that the guy was all in for her. My guess was, he was just biding his time, giving her a chance to realize it herself. Cam was a go-getter type of guy, like his dad, the fighter. He would get what he wanted, and hell if I was going to get my ass beat by that kid for looking at Casey in any way other than friendship.

"I have to head home afterwards. Mom needs me to help with her garden." I turned her down nicely and she nodded, but walked away muttering something about a caveman. Maybe she was closer to realizing things than I had thought. The sound of their front door opening brought my attention dead ahead of me. About a quarter of a football field away, Casey's mom walked out in just her bikini, toward her car.

She was the most beautiful woman I had ever seen in my life. She was perfect in every way. You would have never even known that she had given birth to Casey, by the way she looked.

Her long red hair was down and bouncing as she walked, and her skin looked so soft and delicate. But I knew she was just like her daughter—a hellfire. With a slight puff to my chest, I knew I could handle her.

When she turned on the hose and started washing the old mustang that was in the driveway, things started to stir in my pants. She was so sexy and she wasn't even trying. I watched as she started sponging the car and tossing her hair around. She wiggled her hips to a tune playing in her head and I enjoyed every moment of it. It was like she was performing just for me. A dream come true.

She broke out into dance while getting soaking wet, then suddenly froze. Her eyes were on her husband, who was watching her, shaking his head, and smiling. I saw even from here the blush on her cheeks, as she turned off the water and walked inside, looking guilty.

I watched as Casey's dad walked inside after her, with a huff from my lips.

He didn't know what to do with a woman like that. I would. I know it might sound wrong, but I was in love with Casey's mom.

Read the First Chapter of

The Final KO

Rayne and Arson's story

Chapter One

Everyone loves a good ice cream body sundae

"Does it hurt when you get kicked in the face?" asked Holt, the man I was currently on a date with. I bit my lip trying to not just blurt out that he was an idiot. After mentally counting to ten, I felt like I could answer nicely.

"Yes, getting hit anywhere hurts, but you don't really think about it much when you're in the octagon." I took a sip of my wine and prayed the waiter brought us the check soon.

It wasn't that Holt wasn't attractive or that he was a bad guy, he was pretty nice, actually. He was around six foot, a little on the smaller than average size, and he wasn't built, but you could tell he worked out. He had pretty brown eyes and sandy blond hair. He had opened doors for me, held out my chair, treated me with respect, and tried to engage in conversation with me. I should have been begging him to give me his babies, right?

Wrong. He was too sweet, and while I was sure he would make some librarian woman very happy, I, on the other hand, fought in the MMA for a living. I loved it; it was a passion. My friend Cammy had set me up with this guy, thinking he would sweep me off my feet, but as soon as I'd seen him I had called how the date would go. He just wasn't man enough for me.

The sound of his cell phone ringing brought me back to reality. He reached down into his pocket to see who it was, then pushed it back into his slacks.

"Sorry, my mom was wondering how the date was going." He smiled knowingly, like I knew the feeling of having a caring mother. I did, but she wasn't involved in my love life. I tried to keep that information from her because she was a sex therapist, and she loved to try and help me in the love department. I smiled and sipped some more wine. I was going to have to pee really bad after this date.

"So, I've probably got a few more hours before she will wonder when I'm coming home; would you like to do something else? Maybe see a movie?"

I almost spit that sip of good wine all over the table. After swallowing, I couldn't keep it in anymore.

"You live with your mom?"

He smiled and nodded.

"Yeah, she's been going through a rough time. Got divorced from her second husband two years ago. She needs the company. It's nice though, I rarely have to cook anything." I could tell he was truly happy about his life.

"Well, good for you. I'm gonna go, this isn't going to work out for me. I'm looking for something different. Have a good night." I pulled a hundred out of my clutch and knew that would cover the bill and then some. I didn't want to sit there anymore with the sweet mamma's boy.

"Are you sure? I thought we had something. We could go get ice cream and walk in the park?" He was so sweet and sincere, it was almost painful.

"Unless you are going to lick the ice cream off my tits and fuck me hard in the park, then yeah, I'm sure." The shocked look on his face told me he would not be doing that. *Shame.* I waved goodbye and turned to leave the restaurant. Some of the people looked at me as I walked by and I could see the recognition flare in them.

I smiled politely because that's what I'd been told to do, and kept on walking. As soon as the valet saw me, he spoke into a walkie and called for my car.

"Hey, you're Rayne Jackson!" said someone from a group of teens as they passed by and then stopped. I smiled seeing their faces. I did enjoy meeting people who supported me in the MMA world.

"Yep, it's me!" I exclaimed. One kid looked nervous; taking a guess at what he wanted, I held my hand out.

"Hand it over" The kid's face paled. Oh no, that's not what I was aiming for.

"Your phone. I wanna take a picture with you guys." I smiled and the kid's face beamed—all five of them did. I loved this. The one kid pulled out his phone and set it on camera mode before handing it over. We gathered together and I fit us all on the screen.

"Say cheesecake!" I smiled and clicked the button, then handed it back to the kid.

"Thank you for the picture. Make sure you tag me on Facebook and Twitter." The looks on the kids' faces were priceless. The boys had their chests puffed out like little badasses, and the two girls glowed.

"Thanks! We're rooting for you. We hope you beat Tasha's ass!" one of the boys said excitedly.

"Thanks, guys," I said just as the valet pulled my car up. I waved to them and they cheered then said bye. I tipped the valet, hopped into my little BMW sedan, and pulled out onto the street. I took a deep breath and cleared my thoughts. I was ready to get home, take a shower, and have a one-on-one session with B.O.B. I pulled into my apartment complex and waited for the gate to scan the little security barcode on my back window to allow me to enter the underground parking lot.

Before I even got out of the car I took off my heels; I wasn't a big heels girl. I wore them because even I liked to be pretty and wear dresses and killer heels, but man, did they make my feet sore. With my heels in my hand, I headed upstairs. The elevator ride to floor six was boring and I welcomed it. Once the doors opened, I shuffled to my apartment.

"Oh, honey, didn't go very well, did it?" My neighbor Franny from across the hall opened the door. I gave her a shrug.

"He was sweet, but a huge mamma's boy. He wouldn't even lick ice cream off me," I whined. She shook her head. Franny was in her seventies and was a widow. She had sort of adopted me when I'd moved in across from her, and she was a firecracker.

"That's a shame. Everyone loves a good ice cream body sundae." She turned and went back into her apartment, then was back in a flash with a plate covered with foil.

"Here's some brownies for you." She handed them over and I balanced them with my free hand.

"Thank you, I definitely need these. We still good for American Ninja next week?" I asked. She winked and waved me off.

"Of course, dear. Now go take a shower. Wash that wimpy boy off you." She turned and closed the door.

After unlocking mine, I dropped the brownies off on the counter and went to do exactly what she'd said. I stayed under the warmth of the water's spray for quite a long time before getting out and drying off. I wiped off the mirror and took in my appearance. My straight, black hair was hanging over my breasts and stopped just below them. I always felt like a mystical mermaid when it did that. My green eyes were a dramatic contrast to the dark hair and pale skin. I had a few light freckles that decorated my upturned nose. I looked down at my body and examined myself. I was proud of the body I had worked for. I trained every day for hours—striking, grappling, cardio, and weights.

I grabbed my lotion and lathered up. My fingers massaged over the scars on my right leg a little more, trying to break up any scar tissue. I had finally started to embrace my scars.

A year before, I'd been twenty-eight and in my prime. I wasdefeating every opponent that was thrown at me, and signed with the UFC and everything. It was the highlight of my life—until my fight with Tasha Talon. She was a feisty woman who'd had it out for me since I'd gotten signed to the UFC before her. I didn't have any ill-will toward her; I never cared if someone didn't like me. I wasn't going to be everyone's favorite person, but I never went out of my way to be a bitch to anyone. I was a very laid back chick and just did whatever made me happy. Tasha, however, just wanted me gone.

In the beginning of our match, everything was going perfect, until she had me up against the edge of the octagon. She strike kicked and nailed me in the shin. The crack of the bone was so loud that it was all I heard in the arena. Tasha had heard it too, but wrapped her leg around my broken one and rolled me over to the ground. I was writhing in pain when they called the match. I was taken out immediately and sent directly to the hospital for x-rays. I had a shattered tibia,torn meniscus, and torn ACL, and needed surgery.Just like that, my career in MMA was on hold. I knew people came back from these injuries, but I also knew it was a long, hard road. I knew it would be tough, but I was willing. I had to do it—and I did. I'd worked my ass off, and now I was three months away from my rematch with Tasha. I was looking forward to it—not for revenge, but to show her and myself that nothing could stop me.

I looked back up at my reflection, gave myself the "you got this, girl" wink, went to check that my door was locked, and turned off the lights. I rolled onto my queen sized bed and reached into my nightstand. *Bingo*.

I pulled out my beautiful, blue B.O.B. He was the best battery operated boyfriend any girl could ask for. I settled myself against my pillows and set B.O.B. next to me. I wasn't ready for him just yet but I wanted him to be close when I was. I closed my eyes and thought of my sexy man. He was the same faceless man I thought of all the time. My dream man. He was tall and had an air of confidence that swirled around him. He walked toward me like a lion about to pounce on his prey. I felt my body shiver from his determination to have me. Once he got to me, his hand wrapped around my waist and moved with precision to my ass. With ease he lifted me up and pressed me against the wall with force.

My dream man was the ultimate alpha man, not an asshole, just confident and strong, and when he knew what he wanted, he got it. My legs wrapped around him and pulled his hips flush with mine.

My breaths started to grow heavy and I moved my fingers down to my sex; just visualizing my dream man was getting me so wet and primed. I continued the thoughts of my man pressing his cock against my core, making me cry out. I pressed two fingers against my clit and started moving in little circles.

His lips crashed against mine and he devoured my mouth with purpose. He was dominating me and I was enjoying it—hell, I craved it.

I knew I was building up to an orgasm fairly quickly. It had been a solid week since my last session. My vision took a turn for desperation. Frantically our clothes were scattered about, I bit his lip and he growled.

I grabbed B.O.B. and rubbed him along the seam of my entrance. *Go time.* In the same motions of my dream man, I was filled with cock and screaming my release in minutes. The vibrations and the clit stimulator had me shaking and crying out. When I was done, I lay there and basked in my post orgasmic bliss.

If only a real man could give me the same earth shattering release. I'd yet to find one real guy that could replace dream man, but I wasn't giving up. I would find him. I rolled out of my bed to clean myself and B.O.B. up, then went back to my comfy sheets and passed out.

Note from the Author

Thank you for taking the chance on The Final Chase.

This book was soo dear to me. I have always been a huge animal advocate. Trying to be their voice when they have none.

The stories about the animals and abuse are real. They happen every day, and the general public has no idea. I feel like the only way we can help take down these problems is through awareness. The more people know, the less likely they will do something that will harm the animals. Many people see these cute cubs and want to pet them, trusting the people in charge of them that it's ok and there is no harm done to the cub. If you ever find yourself in this situation. Please think to yourself, or even ask.

Where did these cubs come from?

If they only have them for a few short weeks they must continuously have cubs brought in to remain having the option to pet them on their menu

Where do they go when they are no longer small enough to pet? (8weeks-12weeks)

Do they get to stay there and live happy lives? If so do they have hundreds of cubs there at the zoo (because that's how many should be there if they keep them all)

Any AZA (Accredited Zoo and Aquarium) zoo does no support breeding or handling of these animals. Any zoo that does is not accredited, and is doing wrong by those animals.

Please be their voice. We can help them just from being aware and spreading knowledge.

Acknowledgements

I have so many people to thank for this book.

Readers, bloggers. You are amazing. Thank you for giving my book a chance. I can't thank you enough for being there for me. Whether you are a new to me reader or a seasoned fan.

Susan Bass from The Big Cat Rescue, You have been the nicest person in the world to help me and answer all of my questions about animal rescue. I love Big Cat and I truly hope that goodness will come to the rescue from my book. Thank you so much.

To my Betas AKA Besties. Christina, Cassie, MA, Marissa, April. You girls always help me so much. I really couldn't write without you keeping me in line. Thank you so much for all you guys do for me. Sorry, not sorry I made you cry. Lol

Kiezha, your editing it amazing. I am so happy I found you.

Judy, you rock, and thank you for helping proofread my story.

To my new/old author friends who have kept encouraging me and helping me navigate this book world. Thank you. You are keeping me sane in this crazy business.

Meghan Quinn. You were the first person to read Cammy's first chapter and told me it was awesome. Thank you for being an awesome friend.

Rachel Van Dyken, you are the sweetest person I know, and an amazing friend. Thanks for being you and always encouraging me.

My awesome husband and baby girl.(not so baby anymore)

You both are my world, and I couldn't imagine writing without you both in my corner. Thank you for being the light in my life.

Playlist

On my mind- Ellie Goulding

Animals- Maroon 5

Bad touch- Bloodhound Gang

Hooked on a feeling- Blue Swede

Angel- Aerosmith

Cherry bomb- The Runaways

Stacy's mom- Fountains of Wayne

Peacock- Katy Perry

Marvin Gaye- Charlie Puth ft Meghan Trainor

Animals- Nickelback

Stolen- Dashboard Confessional

I just had Sex- Lonely Island ft. Akon

Arms of an Angel- Sara McLaughlin

Arms- Christina Perri

About the Author

Jessica Florence, Kaleidoscope of Romance Writer of Surviving Valentine. Of The Heart trilogy, Evergreen, Lights of Scotland Series, and The Final Love series.

When she's not writing her next invigorating story. You can find her running her own business, and spending time with her husband and daughter in southwest Florida.

Jessica loves to interact with her readers, find her on Facebook

Www.JessicaFlorenceAuthor.com

JessicaFlorenceAuthor@gmail.com

Instagram

Made in the USA
Columbia, SC
19 July 2023

20515710R00186